**Marcus grinned. "You are something else, Dr. Kara. But I live in the real world."**

Kara glanced toward his crew. "Really? I find it interesting that your contribution to the night's discussion has been based solely on your celebrity. Is it possible, sir, that you've forgotten—if you've ever known—what's it's like to live like a real person? I doubt you'd be able to survive a month living like a normal person. Without," she added with a nod stage left toward his entourage in the wings, "an army of people at your beck and call."

"Is that a challenge, Dr. Spencer?" His voice was low, measured, deliberately taunting.

**Books by Felicia Mason**

Love Inspired

*Sweet Accord* #197
*Sweet Harmony* #235

## FELICIA MASON

is a motivational speaker and award-winning author. She's a two-time winner of the Waldenbooks Best-Selling Multicultural Title Award, has received awards from *Romantic Times, Affaire de Coeur* and Midwest Fiction Writers, and won the Emma Award in 2001 for her work in the bestselling anthology *Della's House of Style. Glamour* magazine readers named her first novel, *For the Love of You,* one of their all-time favorite love stories, and her novel *Rhapsody* was made into a television film.

Felicia has been a writer as long as she can remember, and loves creating characters who seem as real as your best friends. A former Sunday school teacher, she makes her home in Virginia, where she enjoys quilting, reading, traveling and listening to all types of music. She can be reached at P.O. Box 1438, Dept. SH, Yorktown, VA 23692.

# SWEET HARMONY

## FELICIA MASON

Love Inspired®

Published by Steeple Hill Books™

STEEPLE HILL BOOKS

Steeple
Hill®

ISBN 0-373-87245-3

SWEET HARMONY

Copyright © 2004 by Felicia L. Mason

Visit us at www.steeplehill.com

**Printed in U.S.A.**

I will sing of the mercies of the Lord forever:
    With my mouth will I make known
    Thy faithfulness to all generations.
                                    —*Psalms* 89:1

For Pastor Lynn Howard,
who accepts calls from strangers in distress.

Thanks to Lee, Day and Carolyn,
who all know why.

# *Chapter One*

Kara Spencer was running late. Again. She managed to live by the clock with her patients and clients, yet when it came time for her own stuff, she was always rushing around as if she didn't own a watch.

She grabbed her satchel, locked the car door and ran toward the side entrance to Bingham Hall. She yanked on the door. It didn't budge.

"Arrgh!"

Any other time this door would be illegally propped open by summer school students who took shortcuts to get to the assembly room. Today when *she* needed to take the shortcut, it was locked.

Turning, she quickly assessed the options. Was the faster route across the lawn or around the front of the building? She glanced down at her shoes. Fifty bucks, on sale. It wasn't as if they were designer originals. She dashed across the lawn.

As she ran down the hall, she pulled from her bag a mirror and a lipstick, hoping to get at least a moment to glance at her appearance before the start of the panel.

Three minutes later she stood at the door to the main auditorium. She caught her breath, applied the lipstick and shoved the tube and mirror back into her bag.

"Dr. Spencer has yet to arrive, so we'll start without…" she heard the MC say.

Just her luck to have a punctual moderator. Kara pushed the door open. "I'm here."

Two hundred heads turned.

Who in the world were all these people? Kara wanted to crawl under a rock. But she held her head high and made her way down one of the side aisles.

The moderator, one of the anchors from a Portland television station, smiled. "Welcome. We're so glad you could join us. We were just about to begin."

Kara ignored the note of annoyance in the broadcaster's voice.

So much for making a good impression.

The TV personality indicated a spot for her to join three other panelists.

Kara took a seat at the table, nodding at the two men who rose when she approached. She knew Cyril Abercrombie, the local newspaper columnist, and had met Evelyn Grant, associate dean of the college's School of Philosophy and Religion, in faculty meetings when she'd taught at Wayside College. Kara didn't recognize the other man, and couldn't quite see his name tent on the table, but he looked vaguely familiar. His angular profile showed a strong jaw covered in part by a black goatee. From this angle he was striking in a handsome but hard way.

He leaned forward and glanced over at her. Her

breath caught. Handsome wasn't the word for it. He was dynamic in that way all men aspired to, but few actually pulled off. He could be a prince in a foreign land, or the head of a multinational conglomerate.

Clearing her thoughts, she pulled a notepad and a stack of all-purpose brochures from her satchel. They listed information on referral services in town, warning signs of depression and tips on maintaining balance at home and in the workplace. She poured a glass of water and looked up. The moderator was patiently waiting for her to get settled. Kara truly wanted to die. Instead, she smiled and nodded. The moderator turned to the audience and completed her opening remarks.

Kara glanced at her notes, trying to remember if this was the panel about the role of religion and media in today's society or the one about psychological influences of archetypes and stereotypes. Either could fit with these players. Cyril, who had a tendency toward snide remarks, could be a pain, but his credentials were up to snuff on either topic.

Who was that third guy, though? Another therapist? She'd obviously missed the introductions. Kara pulled out the correct letter of invitation, noted that the television anchor's name was Belinda Barbara and that she, Cyril and Evelyn were the only listed panelists scheduled to talk about stereotypes. With a mental shrug Kara settled in for an hour of discussion. She'd catch his name during the question-and-answer period if the context didn't provide it before then.

"Dr. Spencer, I'll ask you the first question," the moderator said.

For the next thirty minutes Kara fielded questions

from the moderator, debated with Evelyn and had a flat-out disagreement with Cyril. Nothing new there. They'd gone head-to-head in dueling op-ed pieces in the newspaper. The fourth panelist didn't seem to have much to say, and Kara wondered why perky Belinda didn't pull him out more.

Then, as if reading her thought, the anchor paused. "And now," she said, "we haven't heard from our special guest." She flashed a six-hundred-watt smile in his direction and Kara leaned forward trying to get a better look at the guy. Why was he singled out as being special?

In her work with the women's shelter and even when she'd maintained an active practice, she impressed upon people the unique gifts each person offered themselves, the community and the world at large.

"Mr. Ambrose, do you think you have a responsibility to portray roles that debunk stereotypes?"

Ambrose?

The lightbulb finally flashed on in her head. No wonder he looked familiar. Giant twenty-four-by-thirty-six posters of the man papered a wall in her sister's bedroom. He had to be Marcus Ambrose, the singer and movie star. Which would explain the big audience and the two TV satellite trucks she'd passed on the way in. Kara wondered if her sister Patrice— Marcus Ambrose's biggest fan—was in the audience.

Kara also wondered how he'd contribute to the discussion, and leaned forward to hear him.

"Well, I find it interesting that Dr. Spencer and Dr. Grant come out on opposite ends of this argument. As for the roles I play, as you know, acting is just a sideline. I've had a couple of small parts," he said with a self-deprecating but nonetheless charming shrug. "My first love is singing."

The audience erupted in cheers and catcalls.

The anchor ate it up, encouraging them to heap adulation on the performer. "Maybe before we adjourn for the evening you'll treat us to a little of that trademark soul."

Kara rolled her eyes and exchanged a glance with Evelyn. Cyril was busy scribbling something in a slim notebook, probably his Sunday column. In a matter of moments the dialogue shifted from a panel discussion to a love fest about Marcus Ambrose.

Kara aimed to get the conversation back on course.

"Mr. Ambrose, what just happened here is a classic example of how we've allowed our culture to be overtaken with celebrity."

"What *did* just happen, Dr. Spencer? Why don't you enlighten us?"

A few snickers drifted up from the audience.

The snickers disarmed her. She glanced toward the audience, then cleared her throat and made her point. "One of the problems with the entertainment world today is that the focus is on the stars, the entertainers themselves, who are self-absorbed to the point of distraction, so much so that the real issues of the day go undiscussed. Unnoticed because they've been suffocated to death by frivolity. And on television," Kara added with a nod toward Belinda Barbara, "the rule about 'if it bleeds, it leads' still apparently rules. At least, it does on the television news I've seen lately. So where does that leave the average American who is just trying to wade through the morass to find socially relevant commentary?"

"Reading my column, I hope," Cyril interjected.

Marcus, Belinda and several people in the audience laughed. Even Evelyn cracked a smile.

"You've proven my point, Cyril. Everything in American society today is about a punch line, a sound bite, a high-speed Internet connection and the fastest drive-through service. When do we get to the main course, the serious matters?"

"I'll have to agree with Dr. Spencer on this," Evelyn said. "As a society we've completely lost touch with our spiritual and intellectual roots."

"And you guys blame me for this?" Marcus said. "The only thing I claim responsibility for is giving people music to come home to, melodies to relax to. Music that makes it possible for them to declare their undying love for each other."

"You tell 'em, Marcus!" someone yelled from the audience.

"Amen to that," another voice said.

"And I find it interesting that you make such a blanket statement, Dr. Spencer. *All* entertainers are self-absorbed to distraction?

"If your lament held water," Marcus said, his direct gaze focused solely on Kara's, "there'd be no need for music or art or popular fiction. Those things aren't necessarily meant to reflect the serious nature of our times," he said, bracketing the word *serious* with air quotes. "Music, art and literature do, however, serve a purpose. A divine purpose, at that," he added with a nod toward the theologian. "In the Psalms, David's many chapters were odes to joy, psalms of praise and thanksgiving. Just as they do today, those psalms and the contemporary ones we find at the movies, in bookstores and even in popular music help us cope with those harsh realities you want us to dwell on.''

Applause erupted from the audience. Belinda Barbara nodded sagely, completely in his corner.

Kara was so stunned she didn't know what to process first. The fact that he'd used the words *lament* and *literature* and *Psalms* and *odes to joy,* or that he'd managed to best her at her own game—and with such effortless style. Who was this guy?

Her mouth opened, but no words came out. She snapped it shut, trying to think of a comeback. Since when did R & B singers know anything about the Bible or literature? Next thing you knew he'd be spouting Nietzsche or Cervantes.

"Dr. Spencer, do you have a rebuttal?"

"No," someone from the audience hollered. "'Cause he's right and she knows it."

Kara blinked, then got herself together. "As a matter of fact, I do have a rebuttal, Mr. Ambrose. You won't find any argument here about the relevance of, or the need for, the arts. I'm a great supporter of the arts. But tell me, sir, how 'Baby, I'm gonna make you sweat and moan' advances our cultural interests?"

The audience roared—people were on their feet whooping it up. Even Belinda let out a bark of laughter. Marcus, himself chuckling, just pointed his finger at her and said, "You got me there, baby."

His smooth baritone made her skin tingle, and Kara got a clear understanding of what made him so wildly popular with women in Patrice's age group— with women period, she amended. And if she did a reality check and was honest with herself, she'd have to add Kara Lynette Spencer, Ph.D., to that number.

Some people in the back of the audience burst into the refrain of the Ambrose hit, and it took the moderator a few minutes to regain control. When she did, she opened the floor for questions.

"There are two microphones located at the front of the aisles. Please state your name, your question and which panelist you'd like to respond."

Not surprisingly, most of the questions were directed toward Marcus Ambrose and had little to do with the topic they were supposed to be discussing.

"When's your next CD coming out?"

"Can I get your autograph?"

"I'm a singer and want to know how to break in to the industry."

Kara sat back with her arms folded. Instead of wasting her time at this homage to Marcus Ambrose she could be at home working on the grant application that was due next week. But, as usual, she'd managed to commit to more projects than she had time to deal with. And it was just her luck that Marcus Ambrose had crashed this particular event.

She glanced at her wristwatch, wondering how much longer it would take to wrap this up.

"Dr. Spencer?"

She looked up. "Yes?"

"There was a question for you," Belinda Barbara said.

"I'm sorry. Would you repeat it, please?"

A young man of about twenty stood at the microphone. A backpack slung over a shoulder and the WC T-shirt pegged him as a student at Wayside College. "I want to know what makes you as a psychologist think that everything in the world needs to be psychoanalyzed. Sometimes things, like Marcus

Ambrose's music, are just there. We don't need a deeper meaning.''

Kara bit down a spark of temper. She lifted the piece of paper that outlined the topic of the night's discussion. "I came here, albeit late, and I do apologize for that," she added in an aside. "I came here to discuss the psychological influences of archetypes and stereotypes. That the discussion veered away from that topic was not in my control. From a psychological perspective, however, there was obviously a need for the community of those gathered here this evening to address these issues. And I'm more than happy to accommodate the puerile fascinations of an audience inclined to reduce the intellectual discourse to that level.''

The television anchor frowned. The college student looked perplexed. From the corner of her eye Kara saw Marcus grin.

Kara snapped her notepad closed and clasped her hands together on top of it.

"I agree," Evelyn Grant said.

For two beats, no one spoke. No one in the audience even coughed.

"Well," Belinda said, filling the awkward space, "are there any other questions?"

"I have one."

The slow drawl shimmied along Kara's skin and settled somewhere it had no business being. She tried to ignore her response to his voice.

"What is that, Mr. Ambrose?" she asked.

"Why are you so uptight?"

Applause erupted from parts of the audience and laughter from the wings where his entourage congregated.

Kara realized her mistake. She'd let her temper get to her. And she'd been doing so well in that area lately. Tonight, though, she'd come in late, rude and out of control—all because she didn't have her own stuff together. That's what came of trying to concentrate on too many projects.

"We're waiting," someone from the audience yelled out.

Taking a deep breath, Kara rose. Evelyn lifted the microphone from its stand and handed it to her.

"Thanks. First, I owe this young man an apology," she said, pointing to the student who'd asked the last question.

He lifted his hands in an "all right" gesture.

"I think I proved the point of this panel discussion, don't you?"

He didn't look so sure then.

Kara gestured toward her fellow panelists. "We were here tonight to talk about stereotypes. We all have them. Many of you hold fast to the concept of a therapist being someone like Freud who wants to stretch you out on a couch and make everything about your mother. Right?"

People nodded. She saw Marcus Ambrose lean forward regarding her.

"The other stereotype people have about therapists and analysts is that they talk way over your head. Ms. Barbara, wouldn't you agree?"

"Er, well, yes. I've done several interviews with psychiatrists and psychologists. I had to get a dictionary for the translation."

"Then they weren't doing their jobs and they were simply trying to impress you. A therapist is someone who can relate to you on your level, whatever that level is, whatever your experience is. I needed to make my point,'' she said again to the student. ''Your question gave me a good segue. I hope you didn't mind.''

He shook his head.

Kara smiled and reached for the brochures she'd pulled from her bag. ''I have some things here for anyone who'd like one. They burst some of the stereotypes you may have about therapy and counseling. The resources available to you here in Wayside are approachable and reasonable.

''Now,'' she said, taking her seat and turning her attention back to Marcus. ''Taking off one hat and putting on another. If you think I'm uptight, Mr. Ambrose, maybe it's because you have some unresolved issues with strong, independent women. Would you like to sit on my couch and talk about them?''

People laughed, and Kara gave an internal sigh of relief that she'd been able to defuse some of the negative energy she'd created.

Marcus grinned. ''You are something else, Dr. Kara. But I live in the real world.''

Kara glanced toward his crew. ''Really? I find it interesting that your contribution to the night's discussion has been based solely on your celebrity. Is it possible, sir, that you've forgotten—if you've ever known—what it's like to live like a real person? Every one of the people in this room has something to contribute to society. Your contribution, though it may reach thousands—''

''Millions,'' he interjected.

''—of people who tune in to the radio, buy your albums—''

''CDs.''

"—or watch you on the big screen, in no way makes you better than everybody else. It's what you do. And what you do is so far removed from the real world that I doubt you'd be able to survive a month living like a normal person. Without—" she added with a nod stage left toward his entourage in the wings "—without an army of people at your beck and call."

"Is that a challenge, Dr. Spencer?" His voice was low, measured, deliberately taunting.

"You can take it for whatever you want, Mr. Ambrose. My point has been made."

"I accept your challenge," he said.

She faltered. "I beg your pardon?"

"On one condition."

Kara looked around, surprised to find that she was standing up with two TV cameras locked on her, and that everyone in the audience seemed on the edge of their seats. What had she just done?

"You claim I don't live in the real world, Dr. Spencer. Well, I posit that you don't, either."

Had he just correctly used the word *posit* in a sentence?

A man approached one of the floor microphones and addressed first Kara, then Marcus. "I don't think either one of you have a clue. With all those letters after your name, you're so high up in your ivory tower that you must constantly suffer nosebleeds at that altitude. And you're just another brother pretending to be one of the people. At the end of the day, though, you go home to your mansion and pool in the Hollywood hills."

Kara's eyes narrowed. "I thought I made it clear

that I was making a point about the stereotypes people have.''

"You made your point," the man said. "But I think I made mine, too."

"For the record," Marcus said, "I don't live in the hills of Hollywood." He smiled. "And Wayside is as good a place as any to prove both of you wrong. I'm here for a month for the music and film festival. We'll use that time to see just whose theory is true. Mine or Dr. Kara's."

Theory? What theory? Kara was starting to panic.

"Well, ladies and gentlemen," Belinda Barbara cooed. "What an exciting conclusion to our evening. The gauntlet has been thrown down and the contest declared between Dr. Spencer and our special guest, Mr. Marcus Ambrose."

Gauntlet? What gauntlet?

"Wait a minute," Kara said.

But no one heard her over the TV personality's voice and the excited buzz in the auditorium.

"Let's give all of our panelists a big hand."

Kara didn't hear the applause. She didn't hear the speculative murmurs from the audience. And she didn't hear Cyril's questions to her. The only thing Kara Spencer heard was the roar of blood rushing through her head. She plopped into her chair.

What had her temper gotten her into now?

# Chapter Two

Marcus signed autographs for the fans, chatted up the print journalists and was aware of Kara Spencer's every move. He knew she was itching to give him what for. With a jolt of surprise Marcus realized he relished the idea of a direct confrontation with her. No one, not even Nadira, his personal assistant—who knew him best—dared challenge him the way Kara had. He loved his fans—they'd helped make him what he was today. And he'd yet to hear an original question from a reporter. Kara Spencer, on the other hand, didn't fawn. She didn't pull any punches. She didn't seem to even like him very much.

And she was headed his way to tell him just that.

Looking forward to the clash, he smiled as he signed a grocery-store receipt. The fan beamed.

"Hey," he said, pointing at the rectangular piece of paper. "It looks like you forgot to buy eggs."

The woman twittered, gushed about his latest release and asked if she could have a hug. Marcus obliged. A photographer snapped a picture. Through it all he kept an eye on Kara Spencer. Over the fan's shoulder he saw someone pull Kara aside, asking a question. Looking distracted, she answered by shaking her head. He saw her say the word *no*. Several times. Marcus grinned.

A few minutes later, though, she tapped him on the shoulder. Without looking he knew fire danced in her eyes.

"I'd like a word with you, Mr. Ambrose."

Marcus turned and winked at her. "Not now. Smile for the cameras."

His face came close to Kara's ear, so close he could smell the scent of her perfume.

Then, before she had time to get her bearings, three microphones were thrust in Kara's face and the glare of klieg lights blinded her.

"So what's at stake in this game?" a curious reporter asked. "What does the winner get besides bragging rights?"

He smiled down at her and in that moment Kara finally understood the appeal of a sexy voice on the radio and a poster on a wall. No wonder Patrice and millions of other women were so enamored with Marcus Ambrose. When he smiled it was honest and focused and devastatingly male.

Kara cleared her throat. Marcus put his arm around her waist and she almost jumped out of her skin.

"We haven't come up with that part yet. You guys have any suggestions?"

The reporters, including ones from the local radio station and newspaper, chuckled.

"There seemed to be some tension between the two of you," one said. "Was that a prearranged setup?"

"I've never met this man," Kara said, insulted that someone thought she might fake a panel discussion on such an important topic.

"I noticed some personal sparks," a female reporter said. "Have you two met before?"

"No," Kara said. "And—"

"Marcus, tell us about this challenge," a man with a microphone and shiny teeth said, interrupting Kara.

"There's no challenge," Kara said.

"Chickening out?" Marcus asked.

Belinda Barbara sidled up to Marcus. She linked her arm through his spare one. "I can suggest a personal challenge—just the two of us."

An awkward moment ensued during which Marcus tried to extricate himself from the television anchor while holding on to Kara. Some of the reporters smirked at Belinda, and others looked embarrassed. It was clear to everyone standing nearby that Belinda, enchanted with Marcus, had lost her professional edge.

A teenager approached with a program in one hand and her mother behind her. "Ms. Barbara, may I have your autograph?"

"Of course." Belinda preened. She sent one final, dazzling smile at Marcus and mouthed, "I'll catch you later" before leaving with her own fans.

Kara tried to tug free of his embrace, but Marcus held her firmly.

The reporters asked a few more questions, which Marcus answered with an easygoing camaraderie. Without effort he'd charmed fans and journalists alike. She, however, was immune to that sort of thing. At least, that's what Kara told herself.

Another forty-five minutes and the hall finally

cleared. Marcus sent his legion of people on to do whatever it was they did for him. The journalists headed to their newsrooms, and the fans went home to tell stories about meeting the great Marcus Ambrose.

She knew not a mention would be made in the media or in living rooms about the real purpose of the evening's forum—to raise awareness about the destructive role of stereotypes. The entire night had been a cliché. People could have been helped, but Kara's message had been lost, drowned out by both her own temper and by the vacuous appeal of celebrity and a pretty face.

Kara stuffed the stack of ignored brochures into her satchel.

Marcus turned to Kara. "You're going to be on the news tonight."

"Unlike some people," Kara snapped as she pushed her notebook into her bag, "I'm not so enamored with myself that I need to set VCRs to view my own image."

He grinned. "You have a wicked tongue, Dr. Kara. I like that. The combination of beauty and brains is…" He paused, then smiled. "Refreshing."

"I wish I could say the same."

He chuckled. "May I walk you to your car?"

The old-fashioned courtesy surprised her. "I'm in a side lot," she said. "It's around the building. I'll be fine. Your staff members are waiting for you." She indicated a man standing sentinel at the door. Marcus waved him on and fell into step beside Kara as she headed up the aisle. The silence between them was not exactly awkward, but not comfortable, either.

"You like that word, don't you?"

"What word?"

"Enamored. You used it twice tonight."

She ignored the question. "Speaking of which, why are you here, anyway?"

"Ah, see, the tardy people miss the explanations."

She glowered at him, but Marcus only chuckled.

"I'm in town for the music and film festival. It starts tomorrow."

She nodded, remembering. "I did read something about that."

He clutched his chest. "I'm wounded. You mean you didn't circle the date of my arrival in your planner and count down the days?"

She sniffed. "Hardly. And you haven't answered my question, Mr. Ambrose."

He steered a hand behind her as they passed through the front doors. "Call me Marcus."

She'd do no such thing. Was it her imagination or could she really feel the heat of his palm right through a jacket, a blouse and a camisole?

"And which question was that?" he added.

"About being on the panel."

He nodded. "We got in a day early. The TV station thought it would be a good tease to their coverage of the festival."

"Tease?"

"It's just a term they use regarding promotion. You see it all the time." He held a hand to his ear as if reporting live from a scene. "'Coming at ten, details on today's bad news.'"

"Hmm," was all Kara said for a moment, but a slight smile tilted her mouth. "My sister is one of your biggest fans."

"Ouch."

She glanced over at him. He stood there pantomiming pulling an arrow from his heart. "Is there a problem?"

"The omission pierces me."

She shook her head. "I must have fallen down the rabbit hole this morning. What are you talking about?"

"You said your sister is a big fan. Since you left out yourself, I take it you aren't counted in that number."

"My tastes run toward gospel, jazz and classical music."

He stroked his goatee. "But you knew the lyrics to one of my early hits."

"Only because my sister drove me to distraction singing it when I lived at home and we shared a room."

"So, you're the local feminist with a Freudian bent."

Kara stepped back, hands on hips. "I beg your pardon?"

"That's not a slam. I happen to like intense, independent women. Strong ones, too."

"I. Am. Not. Intense."

He just chuckled.

"Marcus. Over here." They both turned toward a woman near a white late-model stretch limousine. She wore an orange miniskirt suit, had a clipboard in her hands and a headset phone on her head.

"A little ostentatious for tiny Wayside, Oregon, don't you think?"

He didn't respond to that dig. Kara had been talking about the car, but now wondered if he thought she'd meant the woman. Great.

"That problem with the hotel," the woman said, clearly picking up an earlier conversation. "It takes almost an hour to get out here from Portland. Given the drive-time traffic, we're going to have a very early start every day."

"Early like what?"

"Leaving the city no later than eight-thirty or nine."

Marcus frowned. Kara rolled her eyes. Most working people were already on the way to their jobs if not already at their places of employment by the time nine rolled around.

"I checked out the places here in town," the aide said. She shook her head with a tiny grimace. "There's nothing suitable."

Kara narrowed her eyes at the woman. "We have several innkeepers who operate charming bed-and-breakfasts. And the Dew Drop Inn is right off the highway. The dew *is* pretty in the morning."

"The Dew Drop Inn?" The woman said the words as if Kara had suggested Marcus bunk down in a homeless shelter.

"Which bed-and-breakfast do you recommend?"

"Marcus."

"The Wayside Inn is lovely," Kara said. "So is Cherry Tree House, though it's much smaller."

Marcus nodded toward the headset woman. "Get the Wayside Inn for me, you, Carlton and Teddy. Put the rest of the crew and staff up in the Dew Drop. Rent a floor so they don't disturb the other guests."

"But Marcus..."

He turned to Kara. "Can I give you a lift to your car?"

Kara stared at him. "Surely you're not planning to stay at the inn? For a month?"

"Why not? You just said it's lovely."

"But…" But it's right here, she wanted to wail. In Wayside. In her town. In her space. He couldn't stay here. "I'm sure you'll find Portland more suited to your needs. The Benson and Riverplace in the city are four-star hotels."

"She's right," the aide said.

Marcus never took his gaze off Kara. "I want to be able to explore all the charms in Wayside. We'll stay here."

The aide nodded.

Kara willed her heart to start beating again. She was sure it had stopped the moment he met her gaze and stared deep into her eyes declaring his questionable intentions.

With a shake of her head she scolded herself for falling into his smooth trap, a trap baited with smoky seduction eyes and an easy smile.

She could barely breathe with him this close. Having him underfoot for a month would be unbearable.

"Enjoy your stay." She bit out the words. "Goodbye."

Slinging her bag over her shoulder, she turned on her heel and started moving along the pathway toward the lot where she'd parked her car.

"I'm not really such a bad guy."

Kara jumped. Lost in her thoughts, she hadn't realized he'd followed her. "What are you doing?"

"I told you, I'm walking you to your car."

Behind them, down on the street, Kara saw the limo slowly trailing them. "That's not necessary."

"I know."

Kara stared at the limo. "Do you have a normal car?"

He chuckled. "Yes. It's in L.A. Why?"

"You might want to get a rental while you're here. Wayside is a small town. That," she said with a thumb jerk toward the long limo, "is a little much."

"Wayside's not that small," he said.

Kara snorted. "Right. A big celebrity like you wouldn't waste his time in *too* small a place."

"I happen to be from a small town."

"And I'd wager you don't get back there often."

He leaned close. "Are you a betting woman, Dr. Kara?"

"Certainly not."

"But you challenged me tonight. That was a bet."

"It was nothing of the sort. And there is no challenge between us. I don't know why you kept intimating to those reporters that there was."

He grinned. "I'm going to enjoy my stay here."

He stepped in front of her and took her arm. "The panel discussion is over, Dr. Kara. You don't have to maintain this fierce psychologist role."

She yanked her arm from his grip. "I'm always fierce, Mr. Ambrose."

"But not *intense,* of course?"

She glared at him, then stalked to her car, the only one in the deserted parking lot. She fumbled with the automatic unlock and ended up jamming the key into the driver's-side door. From where he stood, Marcus Ambrose grinned. She slid in, started the car, then gunned the engine and peeled out of the parking area, passing the limo that idled nearby.

"And I thought my time here was going to be boring."

Kara's phone rang exactly eight minutes after the late news started. She knew because she'd been expecting the telephone to ring as soon as the TV anchor announced the story right after the break. She didn't have to check Caller ID to know who it was, either.

"Yes, Patrice. That was really him."

"Oh, my gosh! Oh, my goodness. Kara!" Patrice screamed in her ear. Kara held the receiver out a bit, giving Patrice time to get herself calmed.

"Ooh. Just look at him. And you, oh, my goodness. Kara, he has his arm around your waist. Was that heaven?"

Kara just shook her head as she, too, watched the image of that evening unfold in a spot on the late news. A moment later Belinda Barbara smiled a bright on-camera smile and told all her viewers to tune in for details about Marcus Ambrose's visit and the Wayside Music and Film Festival.

"I am too jealous," Patrice said. "Why didn't you tell me he was going to be there?"

"I didn't know until I arrived. He didn't contribute much to the panel discussion."

"Who cares? He could just sit there and I'd be enthralled."

It stung that even her sister dismissed her work in favor of celebrity. Never mind that Marcus Ambrose had been Patrice's hero and favorite heartthrob for years.

Kara shook her head. "Yeah, you would."

"So what's this challenge business? And when'd you start calling yourself Dr. Kara? You're going all Hollywood now, huh, sis? Today Wayside, tomorrow Oprah."

"Hardly. And I don't know why she called me that. As for the so-called challenge, he said something that set me off and apparently the lughead took my reaction as some sort of personal affront."

"Well, Belinda Barbara said…"

Kara gritted her teeth. "Let's talk about something else."

"Something else? Marcus Ambrose is in town for a month. You're cozied up next to him on my TV. What else *is* there to talk about?"

Kara sighed.

"Is he as gorgeous in person as he is on his CDs and in movies?" Before Kara could answer, Patrice let out another squeal of delight when footage from one of his concerts rolled.

She was eventually able to get Patrice off the line. But no sooner had she replaced the receiver than the phone rang. Again. And again. And again.

The next morning it was still ringing. Had everybody in Wayside been watching the news last night?

Kara fielded no less than a dozen calls from relatives, co-workers and the curious. Then the reporters started knocking on her front door.

# *Chapter Three*

A rapidly growing crowd spilled off the porch of the Wayside Inn and along the sidewalk and street in front of the house. TV trucks and giggling girls holding posters of Marcus Ambrose caused even more disruption on the normally quiet street.

"Coming through, folks. Coming through." A small path opened for the television crew headed for the porch. Right behind them came a woman balancing a large tray of pastries.

"Had I known this many people would be here, I'd have made an extra batch of pecan honey rolls," Amber Montgomery said as the innkeeper held the door open for her while keeping at bay the camera crew from a cable TV entertainment show.

"You probably still have time. These people aren't going anywhere anytime soon." Then, louder, for the reporters. "Mr. Ambrose said he'll be making a statement later today. Over at the college. At three-thirty."

No one moved. Ophelia Younger sighed.

Amber followed her to the kitchen. "So, the famous Marcus Ambrose is camping out at the Wayside Inn."

"This has been a nightmare from the moment that limo pulled up followed by those TV people. Mr. Ambrose and his staff, well, they've been incredibly nice, but what a disruption." The innkeeper filled Amber in on all the details. "What's this challenge thing they're up to? I read Cyril's story today in the *Gazette.* He had more to say about the verbal fireworks between Kara and Marcus than anything else."

Amber shrugged. "If I see her, I'll ask." She pulled out the invoice from her catering company, Appetizers & More, and placed it on the counter. "I saw Kara on the news last night. She didn't look like a happy camper."

Upstairs, Nadira Wilson set a cup of green tea in front of Marcus and picked up her clipboard.

"This place is lovely, but it's never going to work as an office for the next month."

Marcus grunted. He'd come to that conclusion about three in the morning when, with his mind on Dr. Kara Spencer, he'd gotten up to head to the fridge for a snack, only to discover the kitchen door locked with a discreet little sign that said "Off-limits to guests."

"Find me…"

"A house." Nadira finished the thought and placed three sheets of paper in front of him.

He looked at the three houses for rent and shook his head. "I don't know what I'd do without you, Radar O'Reilly."

"Don't call me that," Nadira said. "The one on top comes furnished. The other two don't. The furniture rental place can be here within three hours. The office equipment tomorrow. In addition to a large great room and several bedrooms that can be converted into office space, the middle one has a guest cottage on the property and a home theater with surround sound and a popcorn machine. The third house isn't nearly as large. Just four bedrooms. But it's located right next door to the woman you debated last night."

Marcus perked up at that. "One more time?"

Nadira pulled out the sheet from the real estate company and placed it on top of the others. "This one is neighbor to Dr. Kara Spencer's house. The real-estate agent made a point of letting me know that. He saw you two on the news last night."

Marcus nodded. "Make it happen."

Smiling, she placed a contract in front of him. "I figured that would be your choice."

"Smarty-pants." He glanced over the rental agreement, then thought of the man's taunt last night. "Is there a pool?"

"No, sir."

"Good. I'll show her some real-world living up close and personal." He scrawled his name on the agreement. Then his mind jumped to something else, something he couldn't live without. "See if there's a fitness center here in town. If so, get a thirty-day pass. If not, see if some weight-lifting and workout equipment can be rented along with the furniture."

She made a notation on the ever-present clipboard.

"And get me a couple of…"

Nadira placed two pain relievers on the table in

front of him. He would have smiled if his head hadn't been pounding so much.

Stress. That's what the doctor said caused them. But there'd been no reason for one to develop now. He was here in Mayberry, R.F.D., also known as Wayside, Oregon, about to enjoy a month of what should amount to R and R. A month away from the press and call of Los Angeles and the nonstop flying across country for gigs. The only problem was that he had a backlog of business to tend to.

The good news was that the work he'd contracted to do for the music and film festival would take all of two weeks to complete even though it was spread out over the month. Theoretically, that left him with enough free time to settle down, get caught up on breathing lessons and to unwind a little.

Between studio time, touring dates and video and movie production schedules, Marcus rarely found time to just kick back.

Now when he'd been blessed with the time, the headaches were pounding his head again. He wanted to get a jump on the early applications for the foundation he headed. The deadline loomed, still a week away. That meant the bulk of applications would pour in on the very last day. Nadira had already arranged to have them overnighted to Wayside. They'd reviewed about ten already and still had a box to go through.

He rubbed his temples.

"Do you want me to call Dr. Heller?"

The concern in Nadira's voice didn't go unnoticed. He shook his head. "I'm fine. But just in case…"

"I'll get the prescription filled."

He nodded. "You should give yourself a raise while you're at it."

"You already pay me a sinfully large amount of money."

"And you earn every penny of it. You anticipate every need before I even voice it."

"That's why you pay me the big bucks, boss man. Now, as for the agenda today…"

He shook his head and rubbed his temples again, not really up for the task in front of him. But putting off the workload would simply make things snowball. "I need some time first."

"All right." She glanced at her to-do list. "Marcus, I know we're pretty tied up here, but would it be all right if I swing down to L.A.? My dad's not doing so well and I want to check on him."

"Not a problem."

"I'll make sure someone's here when I'm gone. Just a day on the weekends or when there aren't any events."

Absently, he nodded. "Tell him I said hello."

"I will." She put copies of the *Los Angeles Times*, *Billboard*, the *Wall Street Journal* and the *Wayside Gazette* on the table in front of him. Marcus made a habit of keeping up with the news from home when he was on the road, and he always liked to know the issues affecting the locals, whether he was in a large metropolitan city like Chicago or Dallas or in a one-stoplight place like some of the towns he'd been in while in Alabama and Mississippi.

"How much time do you need?"

Marcus glanced at the papers and at the breakfast Nadira had talked the innkeeper into letting him eat in his room. "Give me an hour."

She raised an eyebrow, but didn't say anything. Normally they worked through breakfast. When the door closed behind her, Marcus let out a weary sigh. He had sixty minutes of peace before Nadira brought in the files of requests they'd spend several hours reading and critiquing.

Despite his grousing, Marcus truly enjoyed giving back to the community through the JUMPstart activism grants he'd created. The first two donations had been anonymous ones to programs he'd heard about. Shortly thereafter, he'd developed a mechanism to provide funding to worthy community groups through a foundation he headed. But he took not a word of credit for it. For six years now he'd been playing Santa Claus, and he loved it. But the volume of applications to JUMP grew each year. If the early submissions were any indication, this year would set a record.

It seemed everyone wanted a piece of the action, whether they knew he was the backer or not. He got plenty of legitimate requests that had nothing to do with the JUMP program. Then there were the diatribes demanding that since to whom much is given much is required, he should therefore fork over considerable assets to whatever cause célèbre the requester named. Marcus liked to keep a handle on where his money went, even though staff weeded out the true crazies. That still meant he had a lot to wade through.

Then there were the résumés and pleas for work in his production company and the songwriters and musicians pitching projects.

Usually he loved it, but lately it all just seemed to

wear on him in ways that made it difficult to remember what his purpose was supposed to be.

Last night Kara Spencer's questions and issues had pricked his conscience. For a long time now, his public work had run far afield of his original intentions and plans. Every now and then someone like Kara or something he'd see or hear would remind him.

And the music she'd called him on, particularly the lyrics, no longer held the appeal it once had. On his past four releases he'd slipped in a track or two that only careful listeners might recognize as more than his usual fare.

Thinking about the project he worked on when he couldn't sleep, he got up and put the cassette tape in a player. A moment later his own voice accompanied by nothing except the piano he also played rang out. These lyrics, about grace, restoration and redemption, didn't fit with the unfinished studio project waiting for him back in L.A.

Marcus ran a hand over his face. He sighed.

Instead of reaching for one of the newspapers or even his fork, Marcus pulled his Bible from his suitcase and settled in the comfortable chair at the window. But before he even opened the Bible, a knock sounded at the door.

"It's open, Nadira."

The door swung open a bit. "Mr. Ambrose?"

Marcus rose at the innkeeper's polite inquiry. "Hello, Mrs. Younger. Come in."

He liked Ophelia Younger. In looks and temperament she reminded him of Mayberry's Aunt Bee.

"Mr. Ambrose, I'm honored that you've chosen to stay at Wayside Inn, but we just aren't prepared or equipped to deal with this. Had we had some advance notice of your needs, maybe I could have worked something out.''

He took the older woman's hand in his. "Not to worry, Mrs. Younger. I've just found a house to rent for the duration of my stay here. It's over on Brandywine Street.''

Tension drained from the innkeeper's face. "Oh, thank goodness. It's not that we don't love the idea of a celebrity here. The reporters, though, and the girls, they're all camped outside and it's been a distraction. I've gotten complaints from other guests.''

He apologized for that, even though he himself wasn't to blame. Then he added, "Reporters? How'd they find out I was here?''

"Well, it isn't every day that a white stretch limousine is parked in front of the inn. We're more of a sedan and minivan place.''

Kara's words came back to him. *A little ostentatious.*

"She was right.''

"I beg your pardon?''

Marcus shook his head. "Just thinking out loud.''

"Your assistant told me to tell them you'd be over at the college at three-thirty.''

He took both her hands in his. "Thank you. I'm sorry we've put you out.''

Ophelia shook her head slightly. "Those people wonder why the media gets a bad rap. Someone's trampled my impatiens.''

Marcus went to the window, but didn't see or hear the circus she described. "Are they all gone now?''

"Goodness, no. But I did send someone out with brownies and pecan rolls. For sale, of course.''

Marcus grinned.

"This room is at the back of the house, so you can't see them," Ophelia explained. "I thought you'd like a garden view. The trucks and the girls and my ruined flowers are outside in front." The innkeeper twisted her hands together. "I don't think the nasturtiums will ever recover."

"I apologize. And I promise to make it right, whatever damage has been done," he said. "The entertainment reporters and paparazzi can be pretty relentless until they get what they want." He shrugged. "Some people think it's news every time an entertainer sneezes. I'd hoped for a nice quiet month here in your town."

The innkeeper grinned. She hooked her arm in his. "You said your house is on Brandywine?"

He nodded.

"To my recollection, the only empty one over there is Mrs. Abersoll's house, God rest her soul. It's a lovely home. And it's next to Kara Spencer's place." As soon as she said it, a sly smile crossed her mouth. "I saw the two of you on the news last night. Kara's a nice girl. And she's single, you know."

Marcus got more than a whiff of preliminary matchmaking in the works and decided to remain neutral. "The forum was well attended and she was on the panel."

The innkeeper chuckled. "Umm-hmm. But the electricity between you and our Kara was pretty intense."

"Well, uh…"

"I know how to outsmart them," Ophelia said.

"Who?"

She jerked her head toward the front end of the house. "Here's what you have to do."

"I don't have a comment," Kara kept trying to tell the smiling reporter. The card the woman had thrust into Kara's hands announced that she was a field correspondent for *All Urban Entertainment,* a cable program Kara had never heard of.

This was the third crew she'd dealt with already. At this rate, she'd never get any work done today.

"Don't be shy, Dr. Spencer. All of Marcus Ambrose's fans want to know what's at stake in your challenge. Is it true that you're the reason he abruptly broke it off with actress Cameron May?"

Another name she failed to recognize. "Who? No, I—"

"He proposed to you last night and if he wins the challenge you'll marry him? Is that it?"

*"What?"*

The cameraman leaned forward, zooming in first on Kara's waist and then her ring finger.

"What are you doing?"

"Dr. Kara, it's obvious—"

"That you all shouldn't be picking on the good doctor."

Three heads snapped toward the deep drawl behind them.

Marcus leaned against the railing leading to Kara's front porch.

"Good morning, Dr. Kara."

She narrowed her eyes at him.

The reporter whipped around. "Marcus, delighted to see you again. We understand you've found a new love."

While they were preoccupied with Marcus, Kara slipped back into her house and closed and locked the front door. In the kitchen she put a kettle on a burner to boil water for tea, then dumped cut-up apples into a cast-iron skillet. Water, sugar and cinnamon followed.

She should toss a load of clothes in the wash and eat a late breakfast, but that grant application still waited.

She'd just put a foot on the first tread of the stairwell when the front doorbell rang. Again.

Kara wasn't a swearing woman, but a few choice words came to mind. She snatched the door open. "I have no comment!"

"All right, then. I do. I'm sorry about all of this."

Her gaze rose and met Marcus Ambrose's. She hated the way her breath caught.

"This is exactly the point I was making last night before the forum turned into a Marcus Ambrose fete."

"May I come in? If they swing back and see me here they'll just keep ringing the bell."

"I'll call the police."

"May I come in?"

Kara nodded. Just as soon as she acquiesced, she wondered why she didn't send the man packing. He'd disrupted her entire morning.

"Wow. Something smells great."

"My casserole," she said.

He followed her to the kitchen. Decorated in blue and white, the room had a country chic look and feel to it. Blue-and-white gingham curtains fluttered at open windows at the sink and behind a table with four chairs. The pattern repeated on the chair pads and place mats. But the appliances and all the kitchen accoutrements were top of the line.

She checked the breakfast casserole in the oven. Five more minutes.

"About last night," he began. "It was great meeting you."

"What are you doing here?"

"I told you. The music and film festival."

Kara shook her head. "No. I mean here." She pointed to the floor. "In my kitchen."

He shrugged, and Kara got a glimpse of what he might have looked like as a boy. Ready to charm his way out of anything.

"The inn was overrun with media."

"And so you led them here? How could you?"

"Mrs. Younger showed me a shortcut."

Kara nodded. "Through the alleys?"

"Bingo."

"Well, thanks for getting rid of that reporter. You may leave now."

"Aren't you going to invite me to breakfast? Whatever's in that oven smells too good to miss."

The look on Marcus Ambrose's face held such little-boy longing that Kara couldn't resist.

He had rescued her, after all. Though, she reminded herself, she wouldn't have been in need of rescuing—and she could take care of herself, thank you very much—if it hadn't been for him. Still, there was plenty of sausage casserole. Would it kill her to be nice to him?

Yes!

But instead of kicking him out, she heard herself say, "The dishes are over there."

Marcus set the table with a skill that surprised her.

She brewed two cups of tea. "I'm trying to wean myself off coffee," she said. "I had a six-cup-a-day habit. But I can make a pot, if you'd like."

He grinned. "I only drink green tea."

"It figures," she muttered.

"Is that a slam against Californians? Another stereotype, maybe?"

"Not at all." She didn't want to admit they had something in common. "You're in luck, then, song man. I happen to have some green tea." She tried to grab a canister of tea leaves without him seeing her extensive collection of teas, greens in particular.

"Song man?"

Kara blushed. Had she really said that? "I'm sorry. It's what I always used to call you when my sister rhapsodized about you. She drove me crazy. She thought the sun rose and set for you."

The telephone rang. Kara sighed. "Who now? The phone has been ringing nonstop all morning. I'll never get any work done."

"Would you like me to answer it?"

Horrified, she jumped up. "No." She snatched up the cordless phone from the base. And a moment later she relaxed and sent a bright smile his way. "Hey, Patrice. I was just talking about you."

That genuine smile, filled with affection and a hint of teasing, rippled through him the way the notes of a new song did. He relished the feeling, even though the chances of anything developing with the very attractive Kara Spencer were nil. She'd made that abundantly clear.

"Yeah, you left them over here. I put them in your room. Okay."

She rang off and rejoined him at the table.

"Grace?"

Marcus bowed his head and said grace over their meal.

When was the last time he'd done that? He also couldn't remember the last time he'd eaten a meal at a kitchen table. Anybody's table.

This felt so good.

"I'm glad you recommended the inn. It's great."

"I told you."

"But I'm not staying there. I'm looking for a house to rent while I'm here," he fudged.

Kara nodded as she chewed. After washing her food down with orange juice she said, "There are several mansions over on Cherryville Drive that are available for lease. The paper did an article about them a couple of weeks ago."

Something told Marcus that the hospitality and truce they were enjoying would end the moment he told her he'd actually found a house, next door, not one of the mansions. So he kept quiet. She'd find out soon enough. And she'd bite his head off then. No need to spoil a good breakfast.

A knock at the back door did that before he had a chance to.

# Chapter Four

Before Kara even moved, the door burst open and a whirlwind blew in wearing jeans and a cropped T-shirt, a riot of corkscrew curls cascading down its back.

Kara groaned. "I'm sorry about this," she told Marcus.

"Sorry about what?"

"Oh, my gosh. It's really you!"

Marcus put down the forkful of breakfast casserole and stared up at the young woman. Then, remembering his manners, he rose.

"Patrice, Marcus. Marcus, this is Patrice Spencer, my sister. Your number one fan."

"Well, hello. It's always nice…"

She grabbed his arm, then let it go as if she'd been burned. "I have every one of your CDs." To prove it, she plopped a gold tote bag on the table and then upended it. CD cases clacked against the table, and several of them hit the floor.

Marcus reached for them at the same time as Kara.

The two bumped heads and then hands. A jolt of electricity ran up Kara's arm. Her gaze connected with his and she felt again that sense of awareness, an inexplicable bond.

"I…"

"I'll get them," he said.

Kara nodded and rose. "Have you eaten?"

Patrice pulled out a chair and sat gazing at Marcus, a dreamy smile filling her face. "I just can't believe."

Kara waved a hand in front of her sister. "Hello. Earth to Patrice."

"Here you go." Marcus handed the CD cases to her.

"I can't believe you're really here. Right at my kitchen table."

He glanced up at Kara. "Your kitchen table?"

Patrice blushed prettily. "Well, you know what I mean. What's mine is hers, and vice versa."

Kara set a plate in front of Patrice.

She helped herself to apples and some of the casserole. "There's a mob over at the B and B. I think they're looking for you."

Marcus winked at her. "That's why I'm over here."

Kara thought her sister might swoon. A playful wink from Marcus Ambrose would provide at least six to eight months of quality retelling.

It was easy to see why Patrice was so infatuated with him. Marcus was easy on the eyes. But a relationship needed more than smoky eyes and a playful smile. Kara, while not actively looking for companionship, wanted more substance than style, more commitment than flash and dash. That's why she and

Howard Boyd made a great team. Howard didn't upset her equilibrium.

With intense dark looks that radiated sex appeal both from his album covers and on the big screen, Marcus Ambrose was definitely the flash-and-dash type. Then there was that smile. Kara studiously ignored the little flip in her midsection when that smile—that Tom Cruise, Denzel Washington, Mel Gibson melt-in-your-mouth-not-in-your-hands smile—was aimed her way.

Since at the moment Patrice found herself the lucky benefactor of that gift, Kara figured it was time to make her getaway. Something akin to jealousy flickered through her. Patrice could get cozy with her hero, and Kara could get back to her laundry and then work on the grant application, without distractions.

She had to remind herself that she liked confident men, not cocky ones, and he'd definitely been full of himself last night.

As if on cue, Patrice asked, "So what's this challenge between you two?"

"There is no challenge," Kara said. "It was just hype for the television cameras. Mr. Ambrose was merely drumming up attendance and support for the film and music festival."

"Actually," he said, the word a slow drawl that Kara found oddly disconcerting, "I was serious. And so were you, Dr. Kara. You were quite passionate in your belief that those in the entertainment industry are a bunch of selfish, self-serving prima donnas."

Kara winced. "I never said that."

"But that's how it came across. What kind of doctor are you, anyway?"

"She's our resident headshrinker," Patrice said.

"I am not a psychiatrist."

Patrice tossed her head, and curls spilled over her shoulder and down her back. "She's a psychologist. But lately she's been spending more time cooped up with books than with patients."

"I don't maintain an active practice. You know that, Patrice."

"So you're writing a book?"

Flattered that he'd think she had the skills to write a book, Kara smiled. But the smile and the good feeling toward him disappeared in the next moment.

"I hope you're not doing one of those female empowerment books."

"What's the matter, Mr. Ambrose, are you afraid that a thinking woman will see beyond the veneer?"

He smiled. "No, Dr. Kara. I'm looking forward to one who has the guts to try."

Something in his tone—a real challenge, perhaps?—put Kara on alert. She sensed he spoke of more than what he actually said. He'd surprised her last night, and he seemed to have more surprises at the ready. "Forewarned is forearmed, Mr. Ambrose."

"Let the games begin," he said.


"See, that's his problem," Kara told her best friend a few hours later. She and Haley Cartwright Brandon-Dumaine sat at an outdoor table on the patio café at Pop's Ice Cream & Malt Shoppe. "Everything's a game."

The two women made an eye-catching pair, each wholesomely pretty in her own way—Haley's golden blond look to Kara's rich caramel. Friends for years, the two claimed to covet the other's assets, Haley wanting Kara's petite figure and Kara wanting Haley's tall, lush curves.

"Lighten up," Haley said. "You looked great on television. And just think what the exposure will do for your programs—not to mention that JUMP grant you're applying for. You could say you've appeared with Marcus Ambrose. And that would be true."

Kara nodded. Getting that JUMPstart Activism community block grant would go a long way toward establishing two of the outreach projects she'd long advocated. According to the program material and the level of funding Kara sought, the granting committee liked applicants to already have established a support base in the community, a base that could be counted on to get the word out and act as foot soldiers.

To those looking in from the outside—people like superstar Marcus Ambrose—Wayside might appear to be an idyllic community, a perfect little slice of Americana. But Wayside had its fair share of problems. From homelessness to poverty.

Patrice was right, and so was Haley. Kara spent more time with her pet projects than she did with some of her original client work. She'd slowly phased that out of her practice, converting it instead into a one-woman resource bank for people in need.

She nodded her agreement, then scooped up the last of the hot fudge on her sundae. "Maybe I *can* turn this around into something worthwhile."

Marcus Ambrose wanted to have a little amusement at her expense. Well, Kara could prove her point and win this so-called challenge.

Haley narrowed her eyes at Kara. "I don't like that look in your eyes."

Kara smiled and spread out her hands. "I've nothing to hide," she said. "But I'm not above taking advantage of an opportunity."

"What are you up to?"

"I just figured out how to best Mr. Ambrose at his own game. He wants to carry out this challenge. Well, he can start by picking up some of the slack on the Adopt-a-Spot program."

Haley's brown eyes widened. "He's a star. I don't think picking up trash is going to sit well. You can't make him get down and dirty like that."

Kara's grin said otherwise. "Then he can help build a house for a low-income family."

Shaking her head, Haley didn't look convinced that either plan would work. "Matt is going to invite him to sing at a service one Sunday while he's here."

Kara wasn't too thrilled about Marcus getting ensconced at their church. Haley ran the Sunday school division, while her husband, Matt Brandon-Dumaine, led the music ministry at Community Christian Church. Since he was a former nationally known gospel singer, it stood to reason that he'd want to connect with a fellow musician.

Nevertheless, she would have expected Marcus to hook up with one of the town's larger churches, one that would showcase him to the largest number of people. With its 250 families, Community Christian was hardly a first stop on a celebrity tour—that, after all, was why Matt had sought refuge there.

"What did Reverend Baines have to say about that?"

Haley flashed her right hand in what was apparently meant as a careless, carefree gesture. Diamonds sparkled. "You know Cliff. He's always excited about spreading the word through any ministry that will reach people."

"And what's this?" Kara reached for her friend's hand, a twinkle in her eye as she waved her other hand around as Haley had been doing.

"I thought you'd never notice." A big grin filled Haley's face as she wiggled her fingers. "Matt gave it to me. To mark our first anniversary."

Kara appropriately oohed and aahed over the anniversary band. "I can't believe you guys have been married for a year already. What happened to the time?"

Since the question was obviously rhetorical, Haley didn't respond to it. She instead asked one of her own.

"Guess what I gave him?"

"What?"

"A calendar."

Kara groaned. "Haley, honey, you're not really supposed to follow that anniversary guide from the card stores. Paper is so, well, cheap. Unless, of course, it's stock options or bonds. And even those aren't worth much in today's economy."

Haley's eyes sparkled as much as her ring. The late-afternoon sun hit the blond highlights in her hair, providing what looked a lot like a halo around the Sunday-school director. "This was a special calendar. It had a date highlighted on it."

Kara lifted her brow in an "And?" expression.

"And that date is almost nine months away. Well," she added on a shrug, "it was almost nine months away when I had the calendar made."

But Kara's squeal drowned out the last of Haley's words. The two friends were up and hugging each other, Kara crying and Haley beaming. Kara eyed her friend's flat stomach.

"When? When are you due?"

Haley gave her the details. Marcus's appearance at their church forgotten, the two women spent the rest of their time together talking about baby names and nursery colors.

That's how Marcus and his entourage found them.

"Man, this place looks like it got lost in a time warp. Talk about *Mayberry R.F.D.*" someone said.

"It doesn't look like Mayberry. It is," another one of Marcus's hangers-on said, casting a glance about Main Street.

Kara and Haley looked up at the crowd of people surrounding their outdoor table. Marcus and about six others stood not three feet away. The woman with the headset and clipboard stood sentinel at Marcus's side, though she seemed to be having a rather heated conversation with someone. She touched him on the arm and motioned her head. Marcus nodded and she slipped away, pressing the earpiece closer and saying, "I don't care how much it costs...."

"Good afternoon, ladies," Marcus greeted them, the trademark smile operating at force ten on the weak-in-the-knees scale.

Haley, instantly charmed, held out a hand introducing herself when Kara didn't seem inclined to do so.

"Hi, I'm Haley Brandon-Dumaine. It's a pleasure meeting you. Welcome to Wayside."

"Thank you."

"If you'd like any information on the town, I volunteer over at the library and I'm also on the historical committee, so don't be a stranger.''

Marcus smiled. ''I'll keep that in mind.''

''And you know Kara.''

He smiled. ''Yes, I know Dr. Kara.''

For her part, Kara couldn't believe that he'd rendered her speechless.

*Patrice needs to come get her man,* she thought, *because he's wreaking havoc with my senses.* She tried to bring up a mental image of Howard, her on-again, off-again companion and escort—he could hardly be called a boyfriend. But Howard's squinting image blurred in her mind with a computer monitor, just like the one he always sat in front of. An IT specialist, Howard Boyd lived and breathed computers. They'd last gone out three weeks ago—to a computer show and sale. It was his idea of a hot date, her idea of purgatory.

''Hello, Dr. Kara.''

She nodded. ''Mr. Ambrose.'' A man with a video camera edged around the group and aimed his equipment toward Haley and Kara. ''I see you're still being hounded by the local media.''

Marcus glanced at the cameraman. ''Actually, he's with me. I went back to the bed-and-breakfast, made a statement over at the college and gave a few personal moments and we're all clear.''

*Gave a few personal moments.* For some reason that statement didn't sit well with Kara. It was as if he could just push all the right buttons and get just what he wanted in his charmed world.

''We're just doing a little filming to get a record of the town.''

''A video scrapbook,'' Kara muttered.

"Yes, something like that." He reached into his pocket, came up empty and called for the clipboard woman. "Nadira."

She turned, and was instantly at his side holding out four slim tickets.

"I'd like you to be my guests at the opening reception for the film and music festival. It's a black-tie gala followed by a miniconcert."

"Why, we'd love to," Haley said. "My husband is a musician, as well."

"I look forward to meeting him. And you?" he said, addressing Kara. "Will you be bringing a date, as well?" His voice clearly conveyed the message that he hoped she wouldn't.

Standing tall, Kara nodded. "Yes, of course."

Marcus fingered his goatee. "That's too bad. I should have known someone as pretty as you already had a boyfriend."

"Oh, Kara doesn't have a..." A quelling look from Kara silenced Haley. "Uh, what I meant was—"

"We double-date all the time," Kara smoothly interjected. "So my friend and I look forward to your event. Tell me, Mr. Ambrose. Do you ever go anywhere alone?"

He smiled. "Would you care to find out?"

Kara blushed and backed down on the verbal aggression.

After a couple of people in Marcus's group got ice cream cones to go, the entourage moved on. Haley turned to Kara.

"What was that about a boyfriend and double-dating? Since when are you dating anyone?"

Kara dropped her head into her hands. "I cannot believe I said that."

"Neither can I. And where are you going to get a date for—" she glanced at the tickets "—Friday night?"

Kara looked miserable. Without even trying, Marcus Ambrose made her reckless. "That's a good question. Maybe Howard is free."

Haley wrinkled her nose. "He's a computer whiz, but Kara, he's…" She floundered for a word.

"Boring?"

"Well, there is that."

"Haley, what have I gotten myself into?" Then she had a brainstorm. "What about Amber's brother?"

Haley shook her head. "He's out of the country. Deacon Prentiss from church can always be counted on as an escort, though."

"Great," Kara said, her shoulders slumped. "Just what I need to impress Marcus—an eighty-year-old pity date."

The next afternoon Kara found herself no closer to landing a date to the gala than she'd been at Pop's the day before. According to his voice mail, Howard was at an IT conference in Seattle. He'd left a phone number where he could be reached, as well as a pager number and an instant e-mail address—all in the event of an emergency.

"This is an emergency," Kara mumbled.

But she didn't page him, phone him or e-mail him.

She was about to pick up the phone and call in a favor with one of her male cousins when a truck backed into her driveway and over the flower bed that marked her property line with the house next door. She dropped the phone and scrambled outside.

"Hey! Hey, what are you doing?"

The truck driver looked out his window and winced. "Sorry about that, lady." He drove forward a bit, then cut the engine, hopping down from the cab. Kara heard the other door slam, as well.

Her carefully tended flower bed was in ruins, the V-grooved treads of two tires running right down the middle of her impatiens.

"What are you doing?"

He held out one of those electronic order processing boards for her signature. "Furniture's here."

"Furniture? I didn't order any—"

"Yoo-hoo! Excuse me." A moment later Miss Ever Efficient, today in a lime-green miniskirt suit, tiptoed around the ruined flower bed. "We're over here." The woman made it to where they stood without getting her heels caught in the lawn. Kara had to admire the skill—and the shoes.

Her gaze was still on the shoes when another set of feet appeared. This one looked to be about a size twelve encased in Timberlands. Her stomach knotted, and Kara knew even before her gaze roamed up the man's body and landed on his face.

"You."

He grinned. "Hello, Dr. Kara. I seem to be bad news for flowers in this town. Maybe I need to buy some greenhouse stock. Nadira?"

"I'll have quotes for you this afternoon."

"My fl…"

Before Kara could get the rest of the words out, he'd motioned to the assistant, who nodded.

"Hello, Dr. Spencer. I'm Nadira," she said, extending a hand for a quick, efficient handshake. "We're very sorry about the lawn. I'll have a landscaper over here to fix it pronto." She then directed the delivery driver to the house next door and started talking on her phone again.

"What are you doing here?"

"I told you, I rented a house."

"But..." Kara waved a hand at her home, and then at—his! "But that one is...it's right next to mine." She pointed back and forth between the two houses as if they might disappear if she blinked. "You can't possibly plan to live there."

"Not me. My staff and I," he quickly added. "We're all set up, except for furniture."

"But..."

"I was glad to see there's a path between the two houses."

Kara winced as she looked back at the winding stone path that led from her back door to the neighboring one. Laid by her next-door neighbor's late husband, the path had linked the two homes in fellowship and friendship for more than forty years. Kara had kept up the tradition when she moved in five years ago. The now treacherous path had been perfect when Mrs. Abersoll lived in the house next door. Kara had checked on her elderly neighbor every day. Together they'd maintained the flower beds that ran the length of the driveways. But Mrs. Abersoll had gone on to be with the Lord six months ago, and her big house had remained empty. Until now.

"So, we're neighbors," Marcus said.

Kara wondered how fast shrubs could grow in place of the flowers.

"So I see," she said, trying to inject some enthusiasm into her voice.

It was one thing to be friendly toward Marcus Ambrose when she thought he lived across town in one of the big houses on Cherryville Drive. It was another completely to have to face him not just on the unlikely off chance that their paths would cross at a shop in town or one Sunday morning at Community Christian, but every single day! Kara's sunroom faced his kitchen. If she sat in her favorite chair, he'd think she was staring straight at him.

He was an R & B singer, at that. Would a band take up residence in the garage, disturbing the tranquillity of their tree-lined street with their practices and late-night musicians' hours?

And even more important, would Kara be able to tamp down the flicker of jealousy she felt every time the able-*bodied* Nadira sidled up to Marcus with her ever-ready clipboard and telephone?

Kara knew herself to be more than able and efficient, but the fact that she'd worked herself into an emotional frenzy in fifteen seconds flat didn't bode well—and over someone whose lifestyle she couldn't respect. She promised to do some deep breathing exercises—just as soon as she established the ground rules with him.

"It looks like these two houses have a connection," he said.

"Yes," replied the conversationalist.

"I hope we'll be good neighbors and can maintain it." He smiled. "You never know when one of us might need a cup of sugar."

"Sugar. Yes, well." Kara watched his mouth say the words, but her mind was elsewhere, like on the lyrics to one of his songs. Something about a cup of love. Patrice used to sing it constantly.

And that's the thought that saved her.

As the oldest Spencer child, Kara had moved out first. Faye followed a year later when she'd married. Patrice and two other siblings still lived at home with their parents. Benjamin came and went as his graduate studies demanded. Knowing how difficult it could be to find privacy in the large, busy household or even to stake out any significant personal bathroom time, Kara had slipped her sister a key under the proviso that she not let Erica, Benjamin, or Garrett know that she had complete run of Kara's place. Of course, their mother had a key, but that was just for emergencies. And in the five years Kara had lived here, there'd been just one emergency.

With a focus again, Kara visibly brightened. "You'll be pleased to know that my sister Patrice spends a lot of time over here. More than she does at home." That was the truth.

She was aware that she was thrusting Patrice at him in an attempt to quash her own persistent interest in him. Since Haley's wedding, Kara had spent time imagining her own happily-ever-after. She'd had a hard time superimposing a groom's face into the fantasy. Until now.

"Well, then, having two beautiful neighbors will be even better."

Kara's knees faltered as if an earthquake shook the land beneath her. Had anyone else felt the tremor? His compliment warmed her, shook her foundation.

"Mr. Ambrose, I need you to sign this form. And an autograph for my daughter if you don't mind," the delivery driver added with a sheepish grin.

Marcus acknowledged the man, but his attention didn't immediately leave Kara, nor hers him.

If she hadn't been watching him so intently, Kara would have missed the brief, though distinct, flash of irritation that swept over him at the man's polite request. Not so much as a muscle moved on his face, but she knew that he was annoyed. It must be tough to always live in the spotlight, with people demanding things from you.

There, in a slight tensing, she saw the reaction he did a pretty effective job of shielding. Her gaze shifted to the delivery driver, who hadn't seemed to notice at all. And now the two men joked with each other while Marcus obligingly both signed the delivery receipt and gave the autograph.

"What's your daughter's name?"

"Aiesha." He then spelled it and launched into a story. "She's your biggest fan, man. I gave that girl I don't know how much money to buy your CDs. And your movies, well, she's seen—"

Nadira appeared at her boss's side. "Marcus, there's a call you need to take."

Kara wasn't sure if a signal had passed between them, though she was sure it had. Those two seemed joined at the hip, and, surprisingly, she found herself annoyed about that. But intrigue won over irritation and she was most intrigued by the man standing in front of her. First his reaction and responses at the debate cum panel discussion, and now this. He clearly hadn't wanted to be bothered with chatting up the fan, yet he'd done it, giving the man his complete attention. He didn't have to do that. Plenty of stories abounded in the entertainment magazines about celebrities being rude to pesky fans and grating paparazzi.

There was obviously more to Marcus Ambrose than he let on.

Despite their differences in lifestyle, values and outlook on life, Kara found herself captivated. She'd have to guard against that lethal charm of his. She'd seen it in play now on four separate occasions—with the crowd at the college, with the reporters after the panel, with Patrice and now with a fan.

On what could only be described as unsteady legs she headed toward the side door that would take her to the relative security of her own home.

"Dr. Kara?"

She turned around.

He winked at her. "I'll be by for that cup of sugar."

# Chapter Five

Kara's stomach remained aflutter the rest of the afternoon. She tried to concentrate on the narrative she needed to write for the grant application, but her mind and her eyes kept wandering toward the house next door. Would he really show up with an empty cup looking for a bit of sugar?

She grinned. Marcus Ambrose hardly seemed the type who did his own baking and cooking. Maybe she'd go over and tell him about Amber's catering service. Haley's cousin, a first-rate chef, frequently prepared meals for shut-ins and folks on the go. For all she knew, though, one of Marcus's hangers-on also did his cooking.

"And why are you so concerned about what Marcus Ambrose eats?" she asked herself aloud.

Finally, disgusted that her thoughts seemed stuck on a continuous loop featuring a certain R & B singer, she got up and twirled closed the miniblinds at the double windows in her office.

Out of sight, she told herself.

But her mind refused to cooperate. It instead found a new angle by which to torment her. He'd said he *and* his staff were set up next door. Kara knew Mrs. Abersoll's house had four bedrooms and two and a half baths. Would all of those people she'd seen him with—including the exotically beautiful Nadira—be living there?

Suddenly weary of her own conjecture and the road it took, Kara grabbed her purse. She'd go to Cherry Center Mall and look for a dress to wear to Friday night's gala...the gala for which she'd yet to find a date.

True to his assistant's word, the garden fairies repaired her yard. When Kara got home from the mall laden with two shopping bags, the flower bed bloomed in a perfect rainbow of color, and two large pots of red geraniums sat sentinel at the edge of the property on the back walkway.

Kara smiled. He knew how to make good on his mistakes—or at least his assistant did.

"Do you like it?"

She'd sensed his presence behind her, felt it in the electricity in the air and the warmth spreading through her. He'd approached silently nonetheless.

"Yes. Thank you."

"It was the least I could do."

She didn't know what else to say. What kind of conversation did a regular person have with the superstar who'd moved in next door?

"This street seems quiet."

Kara nodded. "Yes, it is."

He grinned. "What happened to your long sentences and ten-dollar words?"

"I save them for when the television cameras are rolling."

He hooted with laughter. "That's the Dr. Kara I remember."

"Why'd you move in here? There are lots of really nice houses across town."

"This is a really nice house."

"You didn't answer my question."

"Well, do you want the truth or do I risk another monosyllabic conversation?"

*Monosyllabic.* The other night hadn't been an aberration. She cocked her head, considering him. "Where'd you go to school?"

"John F. Kennedy High School."

"And after that?"

He smiled that too-distracting smile. "Does it matter?"

Kara folded her arms. "Well, if you won't tell me that, tell me why you moved in next door to me. The truth, if you please."

He stroked his goatee. "Because when I found out who my next-door neighbor would be, I couldn't resist."

"Aren't you all a little crowded over there?"

He shook his head. "Not really. There are just four of us here. The rest of the staff is at the hotel."

"How many people are with you?"

Shrugging, he said, "I don't know. Nadira sees to that."

*Nadira.* A nip of jealousy bit at her. "Is she your girlfriend?"

"Are you writing an article?"

Kara's brows drew together. "I'm a psychologist, not a reporter."

"Then why the 'Twenty Questions' routine?"

She shifted the bags to her other hand. "Sorry. I was just trying to make conversation."

"Is that a fact?" The husky tone carried much more than the simple question. "Can I help you with your bags?"

"No, thank you."

"Then I'll let you go."

Feeling awkward and unneighborly, she nodded and moved toward the door.

"Dr. Kara?"

She paused, but didn't turn around.

"I'm looking forward to seeing you tomorrow night."

Too bad she couldn't say the same, particularly when she'd yet to find an escort to the gala.

The next morning, in its coverage of the film and music festival, the *Wayside Gazette* carried a small piece speculating about Marcus Ambrose's interest in Kara Spencer.

A little miffed, Kara considered it just another "tease" to get people interested in the festival. This one, however, came at her expense.

On the way to her car she met Marcus heading to his.

"Good morning!"

"Hi, Marcus."

"Busy day today?"

"As a matter of fact, yes." Then, realizing she didn't want to blow an opportunity, she put her tote bag on the hood of her car and walked over to him.

"You're looking awfully pretty today."

Kara glanced down at the outfit she called her

"boardroom meeting wear"—blue on blue with blue. The perfect negotiating suit. She'd tempered it with jazzy earrings and a scarf. "Did you see the newspaper this morning?"

"I did."

"You've been talking about a challenge and living in the real world. I have a community project you can help with if you'd like."

"And what would that be?"

"A community cleanup."

To his credit, he didn't frown. "When is it?"

She told him, and he shook his head. "Ah, that's too bad. I have to be over at the college that morning."

"Hmm." He seemed a bit too relieved to have a handy excuse.

"Tell you what," he said. "How about you live in my world and join me for a movie. There's going to be a showing of *High Alert*."

"Oh, that's that wonderful Samuel L. Jackson film, right?"

He scowled at her. "No. It's a wonderful Marcus Ambrose film."

Kara bit back a smile. "Oh. Too bad. I like Samuel L. Jackson."

"You like baiting me, don't you?"

"Highlight of my day."

She sashayed back to her car, plucked her bag off the hood and waved goodbye.

Marcus watched her back out of her driveway. "Sassy woman."

All Kara's worries about a date to the gala ended up being for naught. The tickets he'd given her were the hottest ones in town, and when she mentioned to Patrice that she had a set, the problem of a date solved itself.

Now the two sisters stood at the entry to the Wayside Country Club, a fancy name for the town's multipurpose center, public golf course and park.

"Pinch me to make sure I'm awake," Patrice murmured.

Patrice, after taking one look at Kara's purchases, had nixed Kara's dress. "That's for one of your psychology conventions," she'd declared of a silver tea-length dress that Kara liked a lot. Unfortunately, it did look like canapés-at-eight-with-a-conservative-roundtable.

"Here," Patrice had said, thrusting a little black dress at Kara. Unable to make up her own mind about what to wear, Patrice had brought four different dresses with her to Kara's house.

The red one she'd finally selected for the gala featured lots of sequins and left no doubt that she had curves in all the right places.

By contrast, Kara's dress with its plunging back seemed downright conservative. She'd drawn the line at the shoes Patrice tried to convince her to wear.

"I need to be able to walk."

"I walk in four-inch heels."

"Have at it, little sister," Kara said. From her own closet she pulled a pair of slinky Italian sandals that had Patrice reaching for them.

"Ooh. I haven't see these."

"I know," Kara said dryly, pulling the shoes from Patrice, who regularly raided her closet.

Now, standing in the archway leading to the ballroom, Kara felt a lot like Cinderella. In her borrowed cocktail dress and with her hair pinned up, she expected to see a glittering fairy godmother in the corner. But the night was real, and it seemed to carry on it an air of expectancy.

The crush of people in the ballroom attested to the popularity of the night's special guests. Two TV stars were also there, promoting the new show of one and the first feature-length film of the other, a film that would debut during the film and music festival.

"Ooh, look. There's Elena. She's the host of *Celebrity Talk*."

Kara looked, but she'd neither heard of Elena nor seen her show. Patrice, on the other hand, swore by *People* and *Us* magazines and could recite all the latest celebrity gossip as if it were gospel.

"Smile, ladies!"

A photographer snapped their photo a second later, the flash blinding Kara. But Patrice, as giddy as if she were indeed walking down the red carpet, urged her forward and into the crush.

"Oh, my gosh. There's Duncan Jarrod. Maybe I can get his autograph."

Kara didn't know who Duncan Jarrod was, either. Was she really that out of touch? "Is he an actor?"

Patrice looked at her as if she'd just landed from Mars. "His new single is No. 3 with a bullet."

She'd been subjected to Patrice's pop-music lingo long enough to know that translated into the man had a hit that was soon headed to the top of the chart— whichever chart he happened to appear on. Kara decided that she wasn't out of touch at all. Patrice's little magazine hobby kept her on top. Of course she knew all the inside scoops.

"You go on," she urged Patrice. "Maybe you can get an autograph."

Patrice squealed, then dashed into the crowd in the general direction that Mr. Jarrod had last been spotted.

Kara had to smile at Patrice's enthusiasm. If nothing else, her little sister knew how to get herself noticed. Kara had a more understated style. And she'd seen enough of Portland's and Wayside's movers and shakers in attendance to know she needed to make a few contacts and do some networking tonight.

No sense wasting a chance to get a little work done.

From across the crowded room Marcus watched her. The two sisters complemented each other. One graceful and elegant, the other pure confection. Marcus wondered when his tastes had shifted from the latter to the former.

Kara Spencer carried herself like a queen, giving attention to everyone while holding back her own true emotions. But Marcus had witnessed the flashes of anger alternating with humor and the innate caring of the woman. He'd also gotten a glimpse of the passion in her, a passion that simmered just at the surface, ready to explode with the right word, the right touch, the right whisper. All from the right man.

He'd always suspected that he'd know the moment he met the right woman.

All his life Marcus had whispered love songs to women. He sang to them in their cars, in their homes and in their bedrooms. He'd made a career of making women feel cherished, special and beautiful. And he specialized in giving couples songs to declare as their own. Whenever a list appeared naming the top ten singers who set a romantic mood, Marcus always landed in the top five, sharing company with Frank Sinatra and Luther Vandross.

He knew the words to say, the tone to set, the music to sing. But now that he'd found a woman who made the words true, a woman he'd truly like to sing to, she threw back in his face the careless way he declared his intentions. She laughed at his best lines and saw right through him.

Kara Spencer was on to his game. If Marcus wanted to win her—and for some reason he did—he had to reinvent himself. He had to make her see that the lyrics weren't hollow promises and pretty declarations.

Since he'd expressed himself in music as long as he could remember, finding a new way to deliver his message might prove as much a challenge as getting Kara to take him seriously.

How could he get through to her?

Flirting with her got him nowhere. Kara was either truly impervious or just carrying it off well—much like the regal queen she'd first appeared to be. With any other woman he might begin his campaign with pretty words and sparkling gems. The women in L.A. understood the language of sweet nothings and sweeter diamonds. Under normal circumstances, whispered words over a candlelit dinner would follow. That foolproof strategy had ensured that he spent few evenings alone.

Now, though, he craved the quiet—and the company of just one woman.

Why?

He grinned. Kara didn't think too much of him.

He wanted to break down the wall of ice she erected when he approached. He wanted to see her give him one of the warm smiles she now bestowed on an elderly couple, the man dressed in World War II dress whites.

Kara worked the room with a cool professionalism, at times letting the compassionate counselor peek through. She readily touched people, with a hand on the shoulder or by offering a hug to an acquaintance.

Now she leaned forward, her hand poised in ready assistance under the elbow of another elderly woman as she listened to what the woman said. Even from this distance Marcus could see the deference she paid to the lady.

At that moment Kara looked up, and her gaze connected with Marcus's. He saw the quick intake of breath, the speculation and then the cool dismissal.

He smiled. ''You're not getting off that easily, Dr. Kara,'' he murmured.

It took a few minutes as people stopped him along the way, but he soon found himself right where he wanted to be—standing next to Kara Spencer.

''Good evening.''

''Hello. You clean up nice,'' she said.

''And you're a vision. I thought the blue suit was nice. This is spectacular.''

Kara flushed at the compliment and resisted the urge to tug at the dress. By the look in his eyes, she fretted that it was too tight, too short, too everything. ''The party seems to be in full swing.''

''It's a little crowded and hot. Would you like to step outside for some air?''

Kara paused for a moment. Then, giving in to the

evening and a few moments of living the Cinderella fantasy, she smiled. "What a wonderful idea."

The night held a scent of jasmine and frangipani. Tiny white fairy lights blinked off and on like fireflies along and below the railing of the terrace. Muted strains of a pop diva's latest hit drifted out from the closed French doors, and as if from a distance the low hum of conversation could be heard where they stood. "Do you believe in fate, Kara?"

She glanced over at him. "No. Not really. But I do believe in divine order. In God's hand in everything."

Marcus settled his elbows on the rail and looked out over the golf course, his gaze following Kara's. "There was a time when I didn't believe in it."

"Fate or divine order?"

He smiled. "Both. To me, they are two shoes on the same path."

"When did you change your mind?"

He straightened and took her hands. "The night I met you."

Kara blinked. "I don't understand."

"I think you do. You've been fighting the attraction between us."

"I…" She glanced away, tried to pull her hands free of his.

"Why are you resisting?"

That was a good question. One she'd been asking herself a lot. "I've never been starstruck," she said in an effort to explain. "Patrice has been in love with you for forever. All I know about you is what the entertainment papers say."

"You shouldn't believe everything you read."

"Oh, I don't read any of it. Patrice does. And always gives me a running commentary. If your name appeared in one of her magazines or tabloids, everybody in the house heard the tidbit.''

''Most of it's not true,'' he said. ''And I'm not interested in Patrice.''

She looked up at him. ''Then what are you interested in?''

''You.''

Her next words fell away, silenced by his mouth on hers. The kiss first surprised, then warmed her.

Marcus kept it gentle, his arms lightly cupping her elbows. The only other place they touched was at the mouth. His lips were firm but soft, commanding a response that Kara couldn't deny. He tilted his head, and she knew what it meant to be cherished.

She'd been kissed before, lots of times. But never like this. Never with such blossoming feeling, never before with this perfect sweetness. All her life she'd longed for such a moment, such a man.... And now that she'd found him?

''No,'' she said, putting a hand between them, one that at the moment she couldn't be sure if she used as shield or embrace.

''No, you don't want me to stop?'' he murmured against her lips.

''No...'' A jab of guilt hit her. ''I mean yes. Please. Stop.''

He stepped away, but maintained a hand on hers.

''You enchant me, Dr. Kara Spencer.''

Kara shook her head slightly, trying to clear it of all the romantic notions that went with a moonlight kiss with Marcus Ambrose, the famous Marcus Ambrose.

''It doesn't mean anything to you,'' she said.

"This is what you always do, right? A full moon, a warm night. You made a record about seducing a woman with just the intensity of nightfall as your aphrodisiac. I can't be the latest in a long string of conquests, Marcus."

"The music I sing has nothing to do with who I am in my personal life."

She shook her head. "Yes. It does. You're a reflection of your work. We all are."

He released her, taking a step back. "Is this Dr. Kara talking?"

She nodded. "I don't compartmentalize my life, Marcus. I'm the same person no matter what I'm doing. If I'm working with patients or teaching or writing a grant or working at church, Kara Spencer is always the same person. I can't be with someone who has one face and personality on the left, another on the right, one in reserve and a backup just in case. That's too schizoid for me."

"I am just one person."

She shook her head again, and picked up her small beaded bag from the railing. "You've been here three days, and I've seen quite a few different faces. I've seen them when you let your guard down and when you turn on the charm."

"Let me prove it to you."

"Prove what?"

"That I'm a regular man."

Kara laughed at that. "I hate to be the one to inform you, but regular men don't have personal assistants and drivers and staff who wait on them hand and foot."

"I work hard and have a large business operation to oversee. My people keep things running."

"Business operation?"

Ruefully he shook his head. "You have no idea what it takes to make what I do look like I don't do anything. And you, Dr. Kara, have once again proven how guilty you are of the very thing you preached about the other night."

Kara folded her arms. "And what's that?"

"Maintaining stereotypes."

"I do no such thing."

He tilted her chin. "Yes. You do. Maybe not cultural, racial or economic stereotypes. But you have your mind made up about members of a certain social class and profession. And this is all based on exactly how many celebrities you know?"

"I know Matt Brandon," Kara said defensively.

"Who?"

"Haley's husband. He was a national gospel recording artist before he moved here."

Marcus stroked his goatee and looked as if he'd just heard something he needed to mull over. "Really? He never mentioned that. I'll have to ask him about it."

Kara considered what he'd said. "You may be right," she conceded. "About me making another generalization."

He lifted a brow and Kara got the impression of a wolf considering ways to gobble up Little Red Riding Hood—portrayed in tonight's drama by unprepared actress Kara Lynette Spencer.

Little Red had had a chance to mature a bit. Maybe the story would end another way this time. She smiled.

"Tell me what you're thinking."

No way! "It's not important."

"Then what is?"

She could hardly tell him the path her thoughts had taken or that he intrigued her or that she truly wondered how he spent his time if he wasn't posing for posters, singing sexy songs and dating actresses. A heartbeat later Kara realized she truly *was* guilty of lumping him in a stereotypical pile of profiles gleaned from entertainment magazine features.

"What are you proposing?"

He smiled, and Kara could practically feel the trap close.

"You show me your world and I'll give you a glimpse into mine."

"Why do I just get a glimpse?"

He laughed out loud. "Well, I have commitments here in Wayside, but we can fly down to L.A. and I can show you my setup."

Kara smiled, wondering if that might be like the wolf showing her his etchings. "That won't be necessary."

"You sure?"

"I'm sure."

"Maybe that's not such a bad idea," he said. "You could see the house, the studio. I bet you don't ever let the cool, calm and collected psychologist take a vacation day to enjoy life."

Kara swallowed. It was true. But he didn't have to say it—or even know it. "I resent that."

"Because you know I speak the truth?"

"Because you presume I'm an easy conquest."

"Dr. Kara, let me assure you, I don't presume anything about anybody, you in particular."

Kara didn't quite know what to make of that comment.

The end of the exchange with Marcus on the terrace took some of the playful joy out of the evening for Kara, leaving her uncertain about just where they stood. Not willing to spoil the fun for Patrice, she spent the rest of the night nursing her inexplicably hurt feelings and rationalizing the decisions she'd made over the past decade.

Without even knowing her, he'd deduced her single greatest flaw: Kara Spencer overcompensated in her professional life to make up for the failings in her personal life.

She'd had dreams once—dreams a lot like the ones her younger sister Patrice now harbored. When she'd graduated from high school, Kara's plan had been to pursue her passion and sing. She would make a demo tape and then sing the gospelized jazz that she composed and loved so much. On tour, she'd travel around the country and to exotic locales singing the songs she'd written and playing the music she'd composed.

But Kara's dreams had been deferred—squelched by parents who didn't see the value in a degree in music or in what they viewed as an unstable career that promised more downs than ups. They'd strongly encouraged their oldest child to follow a sure path, one that led toward a secure future in education, law or medicine.

After all, as the oldest, she had to set an example for the others, they said. And so she had, giving 100 percent to every endeavor, following the academic path straight through until she'd earned a Ph.D., making her parents proud and giving her younger siblings something to aspire to. Kara was the role model, the good girl. And Patrice, seven years younger, now lived the very life Kara had once aspired to.

Not that there was any bitterness toward Patrice—she loved her sister. But Marcus's appearance in Wayside just brought up some issues she'd thought long suppressed and gotten over.

She enjoyed the life she'd created for herself. But sometimes she wondered if she should have rebelled and walked her own path. Just when she'd come to terms with her choices and the fact that she was single, a virgin and thirty-one years old, Marcus Ambrose had entered the picture, coloring outside the neat lines she'd drawn.

"Those leave-me-alone-and-don't-approach-me vibes of yours are bouncing all over the room."

Kara smiled, then opened her arms to receive a hug from her best friend's husband. "Hi, Matt. And please tell me I wasn't standing here looking like Evilena."

"You were, but I forgive you because you're smiling that beautiful smile right now."

Matt took two champagne flutes from a passing waiter and handed one to Kara.

"You know I don't drink."

"I don't think a sip of champagne counts as drinking." He touched his glass to hers, and a melodic tinkle sounded. "To harmony."

Kara sipped from her glass. "That's an unusual toast."

Matt nodded. "Marcus Ambrose is an unusual man."

Kara rolled her eyes.

"Evilena is back."

She smiled in spite of herself.

He leaned forward a bit, closing the distance between them. "I saw you on the terrace," he said. "And I'm glad for you. I met and talked to Marcus this week. He's a good man."

"Well, you can save the pitch," Kara said. "There's nothing between us."

*Yet.*

Kara wondered at the unbidden thought. Before she had a chance to dissect it, someone tapped a fork against a champagne glass and all eyes turned toward the front of the room.

"Good evening again," the festival director said. "I hope everyone's been having a wonderful time." A smattering of applause followed. "Now we're going to have a bit of entertainment by none other than our guest of honor. Ladies and gentlemen, Mr. Marcus Ambrose."

The notes on the white grand piano started slowly, then built to a crescendo, a symphony of song joined by a bass and a drummer. Marcus sang one of his hits, then segued into another.

"Don't just stand there," he said as he played the introduction. "Dance."

Laughter filtered over the ballroom as couples paired up for the romantic ballad.

Haley approached Matt and Kara. "May I have this dance?"

Kara nudged Matt. "I think she means you."

"Lucky me," he said, taking Haley's hand.

Kara smiled, "Go on, you two. Enjoy yourselves."

She spied Patrice already dancing with the assistant fire chief. But her sister, oblivious to the adoring attention from the firefighter, had her eyes completely on Marcus as she sang along.

Kara placed the champagne flute on a covered tray nearby. Matt and Haley moved onto the crowded dance floor, and Kara hotfooted it to get out of the way of a couple doing an intricate two-hand move.

She edged around the perimeter of the dance floor, heading toward the door. With people from church all around and the attention of a cute fireman to boot, Patrice would have no trouble getting home. But before she slipped out, Kara paused to listen to Marcus Ambrose. He really did have a seductive voice. It wrapped itself around you in a warm embrace.

Closing her eyes for a moment, Kara let the music and the night soothe her. Marcus's voice was silk on velvet, a captivating tenor with an enviable range.

Without realizing it, Kara swayed to the music as if she were caught up in the arms of a man who adored her as much as she loved him.

The piano and the bass subtly changed, the rhythm slowing even further. "This next tune is one on my latest CD. I like it a lot," Marcus said. "And I hope you will, too. Tonight it's dedicated to Wayside's own Dr. Kara Spencer."

Kara's eyes snapped open and riveted on the spot where he sat even as people turned to her and applauded.

*"Your smile is one I cherish. It brings light to each of my days. Your smile lifts me and soothes me and eases my troubles away."*

"Wow, Kara," Cyril Abercrombie said. "You've really made an impression on our guest."

"Don't be ridiculous," she said, snagging another

glass of champagne from a passing waiter. "It's just a song. It isn't about me."

"Umm-hmm." But the newspaper columnist dug in his pocket and produced a small tablet on which he began scribbling something.

"I don't want to see any gossip in the newspaper, Cyril."

"I write opinion, Kara. You know I call it the way I see it. And in this reporter's opinion, that man has it bad for you."

Kara shook her head. "He sings love songs. That's how he makes his living. Remember?"

A woman leaned over, nudging Kara. "Honey, if a fine-looking man like that sang any song to me I'd take it personally."

Kara tightened her grip on the champagne flute.

Marcus Ambrose was *not* wooing her with a love song. He was simply doing what any smart entertainer would do, exactly what all the other celebrities in the room were doing—promoting the newest project to a captive and receptive audience. In Marcus's case, that product happened to be romantic music.

She kept telling herself that as he ended the song. She tried to make her escape from the gala, but everyone she encountered had a wink or smile or something sly and slightly suggestive to say about the song he'd dedicated to her.

"I keep telling you, Nancy, it's the quiet ones we have to watch."

Kara stopped her exodus and greeted her pastor and his wife. "Cliff, Nancy, you have nothing to worry about. Believe me."

"I don't know about that, Kara," Nancy Baines said. "The room is abuzz with speculation about you and Marcus Ambrose. Have you been keeping secrets?''

''I just met the man,'' Kara said in her own defense.

''Well, you've certainly snagged his attention,'' Cliff said. ''Matt told me that Marcus has agreed to do a benefit concert at the church. That'll be terrific.''

Kara nodded. Yeah, terrific. Maybe she'd go to Portland that night.

''I see Patrice over there.''

''Have a good evening, Kara. And don't go all Hollywood on us,'' Reverend Baines added on a chuckle.

As if *that* would happen, Kara thought.

Her head was starting to hurt, so getting to Patrice and letting her know she was leaving was all Kara had on her mind.

''Don't tell me you're leaving already.'' The voice shimmered over her. Kara closed her eyes and tried to steady herself.

''It's been a long night. I have some work to do.''

''Dance with me.''

He slipped an arm around her waist and before Kara knew it, she was on the dance floor with Marcus Ambrose. His hand guided her and she felt the heat of it brand her skin.

So maybe a backless little black dress hadn't been the best choice.

She took a deep breath and had the benefit of seeing his eyes widen a bit. Kara eased away from him, enough to put more than a couple of inches of daylight between them.

''Did you like the song?''

"You shouldn't have done that. You embarrassed me."

"That wasn't my intention at all," he said. "I just wanted to show my appreciation."

"But I haven't done anything."

"Yes, you have, Dr. Kara. Trust me, you have."

At the moment, with his large hand splayed across her back and the scent of his cologne sending her own senses into overdrive, Kara didn't think she wanted to find out just what he meant.

"The lyrics are true, Kara Spencer. Your smile is exceptional."

Kara blinked, trying to get her bearings. Where were the snappy comebacks, or the easy banter that she used to put herself and others at ease? With Marcus Ambrose, she felt about as effective and in control as a sixteen-year-old girl out on a first date with the senior captain of the football team. In other words, way, way, *way* out of her league.

"You've come to a lot of conclusions about me," he said.

"That's my job."

"But I didn't get to lie on your sofa yet or tell you about my misbegotten youth."

"I'm not even going to touch that."

His mouth quirked up. "All right, Dr. Freud."

Aware now that he noticed, Kara dipped her head to hide her smile. "And what did you do that was so bad?"

His lifted her chin with his hand even as they did a turn on the dance floor. "You can't hide that smile from me. I see it. And uh-uh, you're not going to psychoanalyze me."

She chuckled. "Afraid I might find the real Marcus Ambrose?"

He shrugged. "Something like that. You smell wonderful, Dr. Kara."

Ignoring the compliment, but glad she'd dabbed on a bit of her favorite perfume, she asked, "Why do you call me that?"

He winked. "Because it irritates you."

Before she had a chance to respond, he spun her out and then pulled her close, so close Kara could see a single gray hair in his goatee.

"You're going gray."

"Gray is for wisdom."

"And you're a wise man?"

"I'm dancing with the prettiest woman in the room."

Kara blushed.

They spent the remainder of their dance simply enjoying the fluid movements and the music that propelled them. When the song ended, Marcus led her off the floor—and straight into a microphone held by Belinda Barbara.

Kara groaned.

"Chin up," Marcus said, just loud enough for her to hear.

"Well, hello, you two. You're the talk of the ball."

Marcus ignored the tease and launched straight into a thank-you speech to the organizers of the film and music festival, even calling over the president of the college.

"But what about—"

"And," Marcus said, cutting Belinda off and leaning forward as if to share a confidence, "I'm pleased to announce at this opening gala a scholarship for two music majors that my own company will be sponsoring.''

The people gathered around broke into applause. The president of Wayside College stepped forward, made a few remarks and then steered the television anchor to other benefactors.

Kara chuckled. ''That was very smooth.''

''Comes with practice. So, where's this date of yours? I can't wait to meet him.''

Hearing a note of competitiveness in his tone, she glanced up at him for a moment. ''There she is, headed right this way.''

He looked appalled. ''She?''

A moment later Patrice descended on them. ''Hey, hey. That was a wonderful song you sang to her. And I saw you two dancing all close.'' She jabbed her sister with her purse. ''You're just all full of secrets these days, big sis. I didn't know you two had a thing going. Wait till I tell Mom and Erica. They'll never believe it. Did I tell you, Marcus, that I'm something of a singer, too?''

''Is that a fact?''

''Patrice, don't pester the man.''

''You're hogging him. Give somebody else a chance to make a move.''

Surrendering even though the charge held not an iota of truth, Kara held up her hands and stepped back. ''He's all yours.''

Patrice linked her arm with Marcus's and led him away, chattering nonstop. Marcus looked over his shoulder at Kara.

She gave a little wave.

''What's the matter, Cinderella? Someone steal your prince away?''

# *Chapter Six*

Cara whipped around at the comment. "He's not my prince, Cyril. Why does everybody keep implying that we're some kind of couple? I read your article. That didn't help," she said.

"It's the way he looks at you, like he wants to whisk you away."

"Well, maybe I don't want to be whisked anywhere."

"And," the columnist added, "the way you look at him when you think no one's looking." With a sly smile on his face Cyril walked away.

Kara's face flamed. Surely he couldn't see her innermost thoughts. Surely she couldn't be that transparent.

All her life she'd dreamed of being swept off her feet by a dashing Prince Charming. But the more degrees she attained, the more insulated she felt. Kara intimidated men, not by her words, but by the successes in her life. She was a noted psychologist, a community activist and, like Howard Boyd, one of the people frequently sought out to be on boards and steering committees.

After always finding themselves on the same committees and at the same meetings, she and Howard had fallen into a routine: dinner once a week, usually while one or both of them hunched over a laptop or paperwork. Everyone assumed they'd eventually decide to marry, since it made sense. They suited.

Two vanilla people living in a colorless vacuum.

But Kara didn't want to settle for suitable. She wanted color and vibrancy in her life.

She'd done her part by being independent and successful as a single woman. Now she secretly wanted Prince Charming to ride up on his white stallion and take her off to live in his castle. Wasn't that the fairy tale little girls dreamed about? Once upon a time and all that.

This twenty-first-century prince had a white limo and probably lived in a multimillion-dollar home. Is *that* the life she wanted?

Now that her world had been invaded by the very vibrancy she'd once sought, Kara thought she might be having second thoughts.

The next morning those same dubious reflections remained. Patrice was sound asleep in the guest room she'd appropriated as her own, and would probably sleep until noon. Kara had been up at first light. She did her personal Bible study and asked the Lord why Marcus Ambrose had plopped himself in the middle of her life.

She got no answer to that particular entreaty.

As part of her devotional period she read through the commentary on the upcoming Sunday-school lesson. But not a single word registered. And she'd had the same problem with the grant application. She finally put aside the lesson commentary and closed the laptop, her concentration broken by the steady stream of people in and out of Marcus's house. A florist, then the cable company and now from her sunroom window she watched Amber Montgomery's catering van pull into the driveway next door.

So he didn't cook. And apparently neither did anyone on his staff. The minivan with Amber's company logo on the side barely had room behind three gleaming black SUVs and a red BMW. Those, she knew, belonged to his crew.

Anticipating a visit from Amber, Kara got up and pulled out an extra mug, setting it on the table next to a bowl of green seedless grapes and her own teacup. She brewed a half pot of coffee. Sure enough, about half an hour later Amber appeared at her back door and called through the screen.

"Knock, knock."

"Come on in. I was waiting for you."

"You were?" she said in mock surprise as she handed Kara a small white baker's box.

Kara exchanged the box for the mug, now filled with steaming java. Amber took a sip. "Mmm, that's good brew."

Sniffing the box, Kara asked. "Is this what I think it is?"

"Yep. Two fresh-from-the-oven honey pecan rolls."

"I've gained five pounds eating these things." But Kara's mouth was watering before she pulled the string on the box. Excusing herself, she got a knife, forks and two plates from the kitchen and returned to serve them both.

"Whatcha up to?"

"I was just watching you unload while I did some work on this grant."

"What's this one for?"

"Have you heard of the JUMP grants? As in jump-start the community or get a jump on crime? It's a national recreation and prevention program targeting middle and high school kids. The idea is to catch them before they get lured by drugs or gangs."

"Gangs? In Wayside?"

"We don't have that problem, but we're seeing more and more of the homeless street kids from Portland showing up in East Wayside. I'm looking for a way to tie help for them in to this grant."

"Maybe you need to just write another grant."

Kara nodded. "I'm coming to that oh-so-happy conclusion. So, you have a new client." She hoped the segue hadn't been too abrupt, but she was dying to know about Marcus and her new next-door neighbors.

Amber jerked her head back toward Mrs. Abersoll's house. "They called early this morning, very early. The kitchen looks like a warehouse for a convenience store. I've never seen so many potato chip bags and cookie packages. And there have to be at least fifteen pizza boxes."

Kara nodded. It hadn't been an all-out party after the gala, but Marcus's entourage kept pretty late hours on average and cars had jammed the street until well after two in the morning. Kara knew because she'd been up the entire time, alternating between watching a gangster movie on a classic network and

fretting about what was going on in the house across
the way and what Patrice might be doing over there.
Her imagination ran toward Hollywood orgies and
debauchery, so she'd spent a lot of time praying for
everybody under the roof.

She'd fallen asleep on the sofa and woken up early
with an afghan thrown over her. Patrice had obviously passed her as she came in.

"So, is the house a wreck? Mrs. Abersoll must be
rolling over in her grave."

"Nope. As a matter of fact, except for the pile of
empty boxes in the kitchen it's pretty much set up
like an office. The whole downstairs is like that. Except for the living room. That's normal."

"An office?"

Amber nodded. "Computers, fax machines, filing
cabinets."

"Filing cabinets?" What in the world? Maybe
Marcus Ambrose's so-called "business operation"
was really a front for a money-laundering operation.

Kara shook her head. Too much late-night TV.

"What do they have in the living room?"

Amber lifted an eyebrow and snagged a grape
from the bowl on the table in front of Kara. "You're
full of questions today. Usually you and Haley don't
waste any time making the subtle church moves on
me."

Kara smiled and pointed to her Sunday-school
notebook. "That was coming."

Amber shook her head, then topped off her coffee
cup from a carafe on the sideboard. "I'm still not
interested in church. But you're awfully interested in
this singer. Since Haley caught herself a singing
preacher, maybe now it's your turn."

"Marcus Ambrose is hardly a preacher. And I'm not trying to catch him."

"That's not what I hear. You've got the singer part nailed, though. What a voice. And you have to admit he's one gorgeous man. In the dictionary where *tall, dark and handsome* is defined—" she pointed toward his house "—that man's picture is there."

The truth thus pronounced, Amber plucked a small cluster of grapes from the bunch and kicked her feet up on a small footstool.

Kara and Amber had an informal, on-and-off relationship. When Amber showed up with her honey pecan rolls, Kara knew she wanted to touch base and talk a bit. If Kara pushed too much, on either Amber's past or the church and religion issue, Amber simply got up and left.

Amber refused to admit she needed any sort of counseling, and maintained that the past was where it belonged. Buried. As far as an approach to therapy went, it wasn't the best and it wasn't even a formal relationship, but Kara made do with what she had, especially when it came to her best friend's cousin.

"Yeah, he's a looker. But there's more to a man's character than what's on the outside."

"Ain't that the truth," Amber said. She popped a grape into her mouth. "I fell for that good-looks guise, and all it got me was trouble with a capital *T*."

Kara knew some of what had happened to Amber before she'd moved to Wayside, but this was the first time Amber had ever volunteered or intimated details about her ordeal.

Quiet for a moment, Kara gently asked the question. "Do you want to talk about it?"

Amber cast uncertain eyes Kara's way. "Maybe. But not right now."

The admission, a step in the right direction, meant Kara's delicate approach was working.

The issue of Amber's past was a minefield laden with unexploded ordnance. The basics she'd gotten from Haley—Amber's former boyfriend, a cop in Los Angeles, had used her as his personal punching bag. Amber had eventually escaped with the clothes on her back, two black eyes and a busted rib. What had happened to Raymond Alvarez, Haley didn't know and neither did Kara.

In the six months they'd been having these not-quite-therapy sessions over coffee and pecan rolls, Kara had learned that Amber had tried to seek help, but her pleas had gone unaided and unbelieved until the night she'd almost died.

Kara, feeling a little guilty about pumping Amber for info about Marcus Ambrose's house, waited for the other woman to settle into whatever she wanted to talk about today.

"Marcus reminds me of a guy I knew in L.A."

"A singer?"

Amber chuckled. "Sort of. A drag queen. He had a good heart. That's one thing I've learned about people. The heart is what matters, not the outside packaging."

The two women sat quietly for a minute or two.

"It's getting kind of thick in here," Amber said a bit later. She rubbed her hands on her slacks, then blinked rapidly.

Understanding, Kara pretended she didn't see the tears, but she didn't make a move.

Neither did Amber.

Amber closed her eyes and leaned back. "I want to talk about it. But…" She shook her head. "I can't. I just can't."

She got up.

Kara went to her and draped an arm around the other woman's shoulders. "Amber, it's okay to express your emotions."

Swallowing hard, Amber shook her head and pulled away. "I need to go. I have a lot of cooking to do for them. Pasta. And lots of vegetables."

Amber made her escape, and Kara stood at the door watching her make her way across the path toward the driveway of Marcus's house.

*Lord, you know the hurt she's suffered. Bring her peace and guide my words and actions to best help her.*

Amber remained on Kara's prayer list. And during the altar prayer at Community Christian the next day, she added herself and the confusing things she felt about Marcus Ambrose to the tally. Reverend Baines and Matt announced that the singer would do a benefit concert at the church and might worship with them during his stay in Wayside. Kara decided maybe it was time to renew her membership, at least for the month Marcus would be in town, at her parents' church.

Haley and Matt invited her to dinner, but it was the second Sunday, and all the Spencers were expected to gather at home for family fellowship. It would be loud and crowded, and the food, filled with calories, carbs and fat, would be hearty and plentiful. Her mother, whose roots led back east to South Carolina, had never met a vegetable she didn't cook until limp, or a pound cake not made with honest-to-goodness real butter. Twenty-five years in the Pacific Northwest hadn't changed Ida Spencer one bit. It took Kara three days at the gym to work off her second-Sunday dinners at home.

And she wouldn't trade a moment of them.

When she arrived at her parents' home the driveway and street in front of the house was, as usual, crowded with vehicles, including a couple she didn't recognize. Everyone had a car except her youngest brother, Garrett, who at fourteen couldn't wait until he got his own driver's license, and Erica, who didn't know about the birthday surprise in store for her. As a result, the front of the Spencer house always had the look of a used car lot.

Benjamin, who was twenty-six and, like his older sister, well on his way to becoming a multidegreed professional student, constantly brought home strays from college. So she'd grabbed two gallons of ice cream as her contribution to the meal.

"Hey, I'm home," she called when she came through the front door.

The crack of a bat on a ball and then raucous male whooping from the family room told her that her dad had a baseball game on the big screen. Gospel music poured from the stereo system and voices rang out in laughter from upstairs. She knew without even going up there that Erica and her girlfriends were probably on the phone talking to or about a bunch of boys.

Two little kids went tearing around her legs. Kara held the bag above their heads.

"Slow down, guys."

"He took my doll."

"Did not!"

Spinning to avoid falling, she watched her twin niece and nephew chase each other up the stairs. She knew the moment they ran into Erica's room.

"Get out!"

Shaking her head, she dropped her purse on a chair near the stairs then followed the smells of fried chicken and collards toward the kitchen. She waved at her father as she passed the family room. He, Garrett, some of Garrett's friends, her brother-in-law, Wade, and a couple of guys she didn't know sprawled around the furniture.

"Hey, baby girl. We just got a home run."

"Hi, Daddy."

"Your mama's in the kitchen. Kicked us out."

Kara laughed. "I wonder why."

"Hey, K," Garrett said. "This is Mikey and Joe." She waved at the two teens she vaguely remembered.

One of the older men stood. He was tall and blond, Nordic in a way that appealed to her. She pegged him as about her age, and a quick surreptitious sweep of his left hand showed no band.

"I'm Ian," he said. "You must be the Kara I've heard so much about."

She smiled at the lilt in his accent. And a woman could drown in those deep blue eyes. Kara tilted her head, flirting. "Heard from who?"

"Ben has nothing but high regard for you."

"Don't give her a big head," Ben said. "And get out of the way, McGregor. You're blocking the view."

Not Nordic, Kara thought upon hearing the name. Scot or Irish.

Ian looked over his shoulder and smiled. "What he didn't do a good job of was saying how lovely you are.'' A beanbag hit him on the shoulder and he took a side step away from the television.

A smile blossomed on Kara's face. ''What a nice thing to say.'' She leaned around him and addressed her brother. ''You should have brought this one home a long time ago.''

''He didn't grow up with many women, so any one looks good to him.''

The boys and the men laughed.

''Pay him no attention,'' Ian said.

''I never do.'' She hefted the ice cream sacks. ''I'd better get these to the freezer.''

He assessed her with an easy smile. ''It was nice meeting you.''

''Same here. I'll save a place at the table for you.'' She called louder, toward her oldest brother. ''Ben can eat at the kiddie table where he belongs.''

Ian dipped his head. ''Looking forward to it.''

From the corner of her eye she saw Garrett poke one of his buddies, mimicking her words.

''No chocolate fudge ripple for you.''

''Aw, K, I was just playing.''

With a final look at Ian, who was still standing, and with a smile on her face, she headed to the kitchen. Pushing open the door, she stopped, stunned by the tableau. Her eyes widened and the energetic greeting died on her lips.

Her mother, Ida, her sisters Patrice and Faye and a young woman she didn't know—probably one of Ben's friends—were all there, busy working on dinner. A mountain of salad greens overflowed on the island. But what stopped her cold, what shook her foundation, was seeing none other than Marcus Ambrose standing at her mother's kitchen sink.

She blinked and shook her head, sure the vision was a hallucination. But when she opened her eyes, Marcus still stood there. Wearing a yellow apron. Peeling potatoes. Looking as if he belonged right in the middle of Ida Spencer's kitchen.

Details overwhelmed her, too many to absorb.

The sizzle of chicken frying.

Her mother's favorite apron wrapped carefully around a broad male chest.

Steam from the big pot of collard greens on the stove.

The scent of cinnamon and apples. Hand-clapping gospel from the radio.

The testosterone in an estrogen habitat. The adoring look from every woman, even from Ida. The way he seemed to fit. As easily accepted as she was.

Kara blinked again, and the frozen mosaic of sound and sight and color burst into life again.

Marcus held up the potato peeler and winked at her. ''Hi, Dr. Kara.''

''Hey there, baby,'' her mother said. ''I wondered when you'd get here. What's that there?''

He'd invaded her personal space at her own home and at her church. How had he landed here, in her cocoon, in the middle of the only refuge she had left?

She shot a murderous glance toward her sister. ''Patrice.''

''Yeah?''

Kara shook her head. ''What is he doing here?''

Everybody started talking at once.

''I invited him,'' Patrice said.

Ida took the bags from Kara's limp hands, peered inside, then headed to the freezer. ''It's so nice to have the house full of people on the second Sunday.''

The stranger stepped forward with a smile and with her hand out. "Hi, I'm Nina. I came with Ben. I didn't know I'd get to meet somebody famous."

Kara vaguely registered studs in Nina's nose and tongue, and the small hoop at her eyebrow. Her attention never left Marcus. She wanted to wipe the grin right off his face.

"You never know who'll be here for dinner," Faye said as she pulled a tray of macaroni and cheese from the oven. "Remember that time Ben brought those two homeless men in here, with that dog that had fleas? I just always go with the flow. Right, Mama?"

"That's a fact. How you coming on those potatoes, baby?"

"Just fine, Mom."

Mom! How dare he.

"What are you doing here?" Each word was enunciated in the crisp tone of an eighth-grade English teacher.

"I'm peeling these for mashed potatoes." He held high a half-skinned spud as proof.

"You know I'm no respecter of persons," Ida said. "If you stay in my kitchen you work. He wouldn't leave when the men went to watch the game. So…" She shrugged.

Kara just shook her head. Ida handed her an apron.

"Here you go, baby. Wash your hands and help him chop up those potatoes. They'll boil faster in smaller pieces. With so many people today, I thought I'd better add a little something extra. Just in case."

Ida Spencer's second-Sunday dinners could always feed at least twenty people, with enough leftovers for every guest to take home a plate or two.

It didn't seem possible, but Marcus's grin grew broader. "Come on over. I could use some help."

At the sink Kara washed and dried her hands, then pulled a sharp butcher knife from the block on the counter.

He raised an eyebrow at the way she wielded it. "That's for the potatoes, right?"

Kara just smiled.

Despite his best angling, when dinner was served, Marcus found himself between Patrice and Nina, each woman doing her best to tantalize him. Patrice, in a budding sex-kitten way, made sure her long hair brushed against his arm, and Nina, with her multitude of piercings, somehow managed a fresh-scrubbed look that belied the hand she kept placing on his thigh.

He'd helped Kara's brother Ben add two leaves to the table, so up to twelve adults could sit around.

Marcus soaked up the atmosphere, relished it like a man who'd been too long in his own company. Kara might have been irritated that he'd invaded her space, but he was grateful that Patrice had issued the invitation. Knowing Kara would be there, he'd readily accepted.

Gordon rose from his seat and his family did the same. The guests followed suit. The teens and twins were let into the circle around the table.

"We worship the Lord in this house and always begin with Scripture and grace," Gordon said. He picked up a Bible next to his plate and read a marked passage from Proverbs on family and then one from Psalms. "I want to welcome you all to our home.

Our door is always open to you and the refrigerator always full.''

"That's why I like coming over here," one of Garrett's friends said. "My mom doesn't cook like Mrs. Spencer."

Ida turned and smiled at the boy. "You know you're always welcome, baby."

Gordon looked out over his flock. "Whose turn is it for the devotion?"

"Mine, Daddy," Patrice said, pulling a piece of paper from a pocket on her blue jean skirt. She glanced at the singer standing next to her. "I hope Marcus doesn't mind. I went on his Web site and found this. It's a verse from one of his songs."

She sent a wink his way, then read from the sheet. "'I will sing praises to You, the One on high. Your adoration has sustained me, made me whole and sublime. When I sing of Your praises, Your mercy divine, I hold in my heart always a true love divine.'"

Why would an R & B singer have what amounted to a praise psalm on his Web site? She'd heard him sing that song on Patrice's CDs. With the jazzy music in the background, Kara had always thought it was one of those turn-off-the-lights-and-snuggle-up-next-to-your-honey songs. Hearing Patrice read the words in this context offered a new interpretation.

The real one? she wondered with a glance at Marcus. He winked at her.

Kara blinked and blushed, then studied her flatware and her plate.

A look passed between Ida and Gordon. "That's beautiful, Patrice," Ida said. "Thank you for sharing Marcus's words with us."

Patrice beamed at the praise, then slipped her hand in Marcus's.

"Son, would you lead us in grace?"

*Son?*

Kara's gaze shifted from her father to Marcus. She wondered if he'd defer to someone else. But instead of begging off, he bowed his head.

"Father, we thank You today for the generous hearts of the Spencers. We come together today in brotherhood—the Spencer family and the guests they've invited into their home. We come offering to You thanksgiving for the meal that has been prepared, and asking blessings for those who prepared it."

As amens sounded around the table, speculation filtered through Kara. She found herself again amending her impression of Marcus Ambrose. He prayed as if he knew how, with sincerity and humbleness, and with none of the chestnuts that praying deacons sometimes used to sound holy. Like the words Patrice had read, his simple prayer came from the heart.

She'd take a look at that Internet site at the first opportunity.

"There's ice, soda and rolls already out for you," Ida said as she served one of Garrett's friends a double helping of mashed potatoes. "And I made a salad for you. You all make sure to eat something green."

"Yes, ma'am."

"I want a chicken leg, Gramma," one of the twins said.

"Here you go, baby."

After filling their plates, the teenagers and kids retreated to the family room, where card tables had been set up for them. As bowls and platters were passed around, Marcus kept up a steady stream of banter with his pretty dinner companions. As the meal progressed, they each did their best to woo him. His attention, however, remained riveted on Kara.

She sat across the table, making goo-goo eyes with McGregor. Women always fell for those phony James Bond accents. Unfortunately, McGregor's was real.

"Me Mum is Irish with some Scots tossed in for good measure, but me Da is from Edinburgh. That's where I grew up."

"So you're working on your doctorate here?"

He nodded around a bite of food. "In economics. Met your brother on the quad. Playing soccer."

"I love soccer."

"Then we'll have to go to a match together. How about this weekend? Saturday?"

She started to decline the date, then saw Marcus scowl at her. "I'd love to."

Ian beamed.

"So you're working on the big one, eh? Our Kara has a Ph.D.," Gordon Spencer said from the head of the table. "She's a headshrinker."

"Daddy."

"She's a psychologist, Dad," Patrice piped up. "There's a difference."

Gordon grunted. "Hundred fifty an hour is a head-shrinker to me. But she does a lot of grant writing and work at her church," he added, focusing first on Ian, then on Marcus. "We're right proud of her."

Marcus raised his glass of ginger ale at her.

"Dad, you're embarrassing me."

His broad smile carried parental pride. "Nothing to be embarrassed about. You're a good girl."

"So, Ian," Kara said, "what do you plan to do after you complete the dissertation?"

Marcus didn't have time to feel summarily dismissed. He leaned forward trying to hear the hushed words between Ian and Kara, who'd bent their heads together.

"We've waited long enough, Marcus," Faye said as she passed a basket of rolls to her husband. "Mama told us not to pounce on you, but you know we have a million questions."

"When's your next movie coming out? I loved *High Alert*. And I can't wait for that new disc. I read in the paper that you sang a song from it Friday night."

He answered their questions, aware that Ida and Gordon and just about everyone else at the table hung on his words. Everyone except Kara, who was too busy flirting with McGregor.

When it came time for dessert, the women cleared the dishes while Ida and Kara went to the kitchen. They returned with a tray of bowls, spoons, one of the ice cream containers and two apple pies.

"A man could get used to pulling up at your table, Mrs. Spencer," Marcus said.

Ian nodded. "I agree with him," he said, patting his stomach. "I've never had a meal so fine."

Kara scooped out ice cream and passed plates to Ian, who sent them around. She added an extra portion to Ian's and slighted Marcus. He just smiled and handed the bowl to Ida, who shook her head and took over scooping duties.

"Did you all know that Marcus is living right next

door to Kara?'' Patrice's question stopped all conversation around the table. Everyone looked at Kara, then at Marcus.

Faye exchanged a sly look with her husband.

''Well, isn't that nice.''

''The house was available,'' Marcus said.

As people finished up and drifted away from the table, Kara and her sisters headed to the kitchen.

''Mom, you go rest. We'll clean up in here,'' Kara said as she tugged down the dishwasher door.

''It's on the fritz,'' Ida said. ''So don't put them in there. Just stack them in the sink and I'll take care of them later.''

''That's okay, Mom. I'll do them.'' She shooed her out. ''Go put your feet up. Enjoy the afternoon.''

''That's right, Mrs. Spencer. I'll help Kara.''

Kara considered Marcus for a moment. Then she nodded reluctantly. ''All right.''

''I'll help, too,'' Patrice said.

''Not so fast, missy,'' Ida called. ''I need to talk to you. And Faye, I love my grandbabies to pieces, but if those kids tear up my living room, there are gonna be some words and more than a time-out.''

''I'll check on them, Mom.''

''Come on, Patrice. Kara and Marcus have things under control in here.'' Patrice pouted, but followed her mother. Faye trailed behind them, but at the door turned and gave Kara a thumbs-up.

Kara ran water into the sink, adding dish detergent, then started on the plates. They worked in silence for a few minutes, Kara glancing up at him every now and then.

''You're not what you appear to be,'' she said.

A shadow smile creased his mouth. "Most people aren't."

Rinsing the plate, he then dried it. "So, are you serious about that McGregor fellow?"

"We have a lot in common."

"So do we," Marcus said.

"Like what?"

He dipped his hand in the soapy water and ran the suds up her arm. "Attitude. And outlook. Green tea. We want the same things. We just go about getting them in different ways."

"You don't know what I want."

He smiled. "Yeah, I do. You're an accomplished woman, well respected in the community. Adored at home. But something's missing," he said. "I see it in your eyes."

Kara looked away, busied herself with forks and spoons.

"Don't go out with him," Marcus said. "Go out with me."

Kara opened her mouth, but no words came out.

"Please."

All the reasons not to rushed through her head. And leading the list—"Patrice…"

"Can find her own date."

"I gave him my word."

He couldn't argue with that. "Then go out with me after your date with him. You can watch him play soccer and then escape when he goes into the locker room."

Kara laughed. "Aren't you being a little childish?"

He shrugged and looked away. Kara marveled. Had she just glimpsed a touch of jealousy?

# *Chapter Seven*

That couldn't be the case. He was, after all, Marcus Ambrose. The star who could get anyone or anything he wanted. Wasn't he dating a supermodel or actress or something back in L.A.?

"I can't go out with you," she said.

"Why?"

"Well, because…" Kara paused, realizing that she really didn't have an answer or a because. "I'm sure Patrice would be happy to show you around."

"I'd prefer your perspective."

"Why?" The question came out before she could suppress it.

Embarrassed and not used to such dogged intensity, Kara looked away and plunged her hand into the dishwater. The dish he was drying slipped out of his hand at the sudden move. As he reached to scoop it out of the water, he grabbed something definitely un-plate-like.

Kara tensed. Her gaze flew to his, then to their joined hands in the warm water.

He laced his fingers with hers and Kara forgot to breathe.

"Wh-what are you doing?"

"Helping you wash dishes."

"You're supposed to dry."

"Maybe I want a new experience."

Kara's eyes met his.

He leaned forward, giving her time to move away.

She didn't. She knew what was coming and she wanted to savor the sweetness of his kiss again. She might regret it later, but right now was all that mattered.

His lips touched hers like a whisper. Closing her eyes, Kara gave herself up to the moment. All the emotions she'd tried to suppress were overtaken by the quiet pleasure of his gentle touch.

He brought their hands up from the dishwater.

"We'd better finish this," he said.

Kara wondered if he meant the dishes or the kisses.

Truth be told, she wanted it to be the latter. But given the sheer volume of the task in front of them, she turned her attention back to the dishes. It took a while to complete their chore. When they did, Kara wiped down the countertop and the range, then dried her hands.

"I hope you didn't feel too overwhelmed by everybody today."

"Not at all. I enjoyed myself. Your folks are good people."

She nodded, agreeing with that. "But my family, collectively, can be...all over a person." She'd started to say cloying, but didn't want to give him the impression that she didn't like her family. She did. At the same time she knew how overwhelming they could be. "Things can get rather suffocating if you're not careful."

"Is that why you moved out?"

Startled, she regarded him. "I—I never thought about it that way. It was just time. And I got a great interest rate and deal on the house. With me gone, and Faye married and gone, that freed up a bedroom here so everybody else could spread out a little."

He smiled.

"What?"

"You're very lucky to have such a large, close-knit family."

She took the towel from his hands and draped it over the oven handle to dry. "You wouldn't say that if you were fourth or fifth in line to get in the bathroom."

"What is it about women and their bathrooms?"

She tapped him on the shoulder as she walked by. "It's a female thing. One of our closely guarded secrets."

In the family room a young real estate mogul by the name of Garrett Spencer whipped the pants off all the other players, demanding exorbitant rent each time they landed on property he owned.

"Come on over here, Marcus," Gordon called. "I was just about to put in a video of when Kara graduated."

"Daddy, I'm sure Marcus isn't interested in that."

"Actually, it sounds intriguing," Marcus said.

Gordon looked up from the rows and rows of videocassette cases in shelving next to the big-screen television. "Well, here's a better one," he said.

Kara breathed a sigh of relief until the images

came up and she saw herself clutching a hairbrush in one hand. A white T-shirt pulled over her head served as a long-haired wig.

She groaned.

"Ooh, ooh. Check it out," Garrett said, poking his friends. "This is Kara doing her diva act."

Marcus raised an eyebrow. Ida patted the cushion next to her on the sofa, one of three that formed a U in front of the television, inviting Marcus to get comfortable. "This is funny," she said.

"I'm leaving."

"Oh, no, you don't," Faye said, grabbing Kara and pulling her down next to her on a large ottoman. "I'm not going to be embarrassed by myself."

On the video a much younger Kara belted out "R-E-S-P-E-C-T," while Faye jumped around playing air guitar and phantom piano behind her. Ben's image blurred in and out and then focused. Two long wooden spoons served as drumsticks as he beat out a rhythm on the dresser top.

"See, this is why I stay on campus," Ben told his friends.

"Thank the good Lord the parents got over this video-camera thing by the time we came along," Erica said.

"Don't bet on it," Ben said to the youngest Spencers. "There're plenty of blackmail tapes on you two."

On the video Kara segued into a soulful Billie Holiday tune and her brother and sister took up the doo-wop duo role. Faye's twins shimmied in front of the TV, following the moves on the video. Kara closed out with a gospel tribute to the late great Mahalia Jackson.

Ida nodded toward the upright piano. Marcus nodded back, and slipped away and onto the bench. As Kara sang on the video, he started playing the same song. It didn't take long for the Spencers and their guests to surround him joining in a sing-along.

Hanging back, Kara studied him. Marcus Ambrose had appeal, all right. He'd managed, yet again, to shift the focus so the spotlight—tonight in the form of her family's attention—remained shining on him. He'd done it so effortlessly, she wondered if he even realized it.

She'd seen a trace of a man who put others first, but mostly Marcus Ambrose proved the point she'd made at the panel discussion—high-maintenance, self-absorbed celebrities like Marcus Ambrose couldn't function without constant and fawning attention.

The next day, after she'd done her rounds at the senior citizens building next door to her office in the community resource center and checked in at the women's shelter where she volunteered, Kara pulled into her driveway looking forward to a hot bath and a relaxing evening. The messages she found waiting on her answering machine stunned, then angered her. She looked across the stone pathway at Marcus's house. Two of the SUVs were there.

She marched across the way and rapped on his back door. Expecting his assistant Nadira, Kara was surprised when Marcus came to the door, barefoot and wearing jeans and a shirt that wasn't buttoned.

For a moment Kara forgot what she'd come over for. Up close and this personal was a completely different game. She'd seen plenty of posters of him, but nothing had prepared her for this. He radiated leashed strength, and she felt a confusing blend of sensations. Curiosity. Fear. And something more than interest.

"Howdy, neighbor."

With effort, she dragged her gaze to his face. Mistake. The lazy smile beckoned, the one that teased fans into buying his music, posters and other merchandise. Was there no part of this man that didn't discombobulate her?

Closing her eyes for a moment, Kara marshaled her defenses and focused on the reason she'd come to face him.

"You don't have to curry favor with my parents. They already like you."

"I wasn't doing that."

Hands went to hips. "Then why did a brand-new dishwasher arrive at my mother's house today?"

"Because hers was broken." Lounging against the doorjamb, he said the words as if any six-year-old would understand the logic.

"Did it ever occur to you that maybe I, or we— my brothers and sisters—might want to do that for her?"

He reached for her hand. "I didn't mean to spoil your plans."

The warmth of his hand enveloped her. She stared at it even as his words registered. He sounded so genuinely contrite that Kara felt bad. "You didn't," she conceded. When his smile broadened, she snatched her hand away, adding, "But you could have."

"Your parents were wonderful to me. I just

wanted to show them kindness.'' He tilted her chin up. ''Don't be angry with me, Dr. Kara.''

''Stop calling me that.''

''All right. Don't be angry, honey.''

''You're impossible.''

''Where would you like to go Saturday night?''

''I can't go out with you Saturday. I promised that day to Ian. You know that.''

Marcus rolled his eyes, but wasn't dissuaded. ''Then have dinner with me Friday night.''

''Aren't you supposed to be doing something at the college with the festival? You know,'' she said, snapping her fingers as if that would help him recall. ''The reason you're *in* Wayside. I don't think contracts with the college included a clause about pestering me.''

His face scrunched up as if he was in pain. ''Oh, man. I forgot about that.''

Kara chuckled. ''Oh, well. See you later.''

He grabbed her arm as she turned to go. ''Afterward, then. Go out with me after the master class.''

''Don't you ever give up?''

''Not when it's something I want.''

Kara's breath caught. She swallowed involuntarily, and met his gaze straight on.

''Why are you so intent on this? There are lots of women in town who'd jump at the chance to be with you.''

''That's why,'' he said. ''I've never met anyone like you. Someone who wasn't impressed with what I do.''

''I'm supposed to be impressed?''

Shaking his head, he tried to clarify. ''No. But a lot of people just see the trappings, the notoriety and all that it brings. They like it and want to be a part of it. You, on the other hand, don't pay any attention to any of that stuff.''

She looked at him and then away, not sure how to take the words that could have been a compliment. She turned to go and he called after her again.

''Hey, Kara?''

''Yes,'' she said over her shoulder.

''You have a great voice.''

The compliment swirled inside her, blossoming into a smile on her lips.

''I'm looking forward to Friday night,'' he said.

So was she.

When Kara left for work Friday morning, a laminated pass perched on the window shield of her car. Not a single vehicle sat at Marcus's house, but closer inspection of the card on a clip chain showed her that it gave her total access to all of the events during the music and film festival.

Kara laughed out loud. ''So now I'm with the band.''

In the evening, though, her stomach was in knots. After changing clothes three times, she settled on a sleeveless red shift and her favorite pair of shoes. A final glance in the mirror let her know she did, indeed, look good.

Into a matching bag she tucked her driver's license, a lipstick, a credit card and forty bucks of just-in-case cash. After she shut and locked the house door and turned toward her car she saw the limousine. Both the white car and the chauffeur standing beside it looked out of place on her quiet, residential street.

"Good evening, Dr. Spencer," he said as he opened the door.

"This is for me?"

"Yes, ma'am. My name is Carlton. Let me know if I can be of any service to you."

Kara grinned. Going out with Marcus Ambrose did have its perks. She'd never been in a limo before.

"You have your festival pass, ma'am?"

She found the deference a little disconcerting. *Ma'am.* At thirty-one, she hardly qualified. Even her mother, who'd maintained her Southern ways and accent and had never met a person she didn't call "sugar," "honey," or "baby," would balk at "ma'am."

Kara nodded and held up the four-by-six-inch card that would give her backstage access.

"You'll need to wear it," he said as he opened the door for her.

Kara started to object that the thing didn't match her carefully chosen outfit. Its big lettering, logo and that yellow corded chain could hardly be termed a fashion accessory. Keeping her thoughts to herself, she slipped into the buttery soft leather of the limousine.

Was this his personal car or a rental?

She wiggled in the seat, enjoying the luxury, then looked around at all of the accoutrements. That's when she noticed the rose. A single long-stemmed bud. Not red. That would have been cliché. Kara reached for the stem. The white rose had just a touch of pink at the rim.

Settling into the soft leather, with the flower at her nose, Kara smiled in spite of herself. She was really going on a date with Marcus Ambrose.

The drive to the college was short. When Kara slipped into the small auditorium that held his master class, Marcus paused right in the middle of his presentation. A smile lit up his face.

"Hi."

Kara, wondering if she'd ever again make an appearance at Wayside College without being terminally embarrassed, gave a little wave and tried to sit in one of the two empty seats in the last row. But Marcus wasn't having it.

"Just a sec," he told the music students, who all turned to see what had captured his attention as he bounded up the dozen or so wide stairs. He took Kara's hand.

"Come on. I saved a seat for you."

The people in the class chuckled as he led Kara to the very first row.

The crowd of about ninety was mixed, mostly graduate students, but a few gifted and talented kids from Wayside High sat in, as well.

"This is Dr. Kara," he told the group.

He lifted a hand as if directing and pointed a finger at the students. As if on cue, the master class echoed, "Hi, Dr. Kara."

She waved back, half covering her face with her hands in mock embarrassment. Marcus chuckled, then turned his attention back to his presentation, settling himself on the high stool.

The moderator looked uncomfortable in his clothing, an outfit of black on black that tried to pull off an artistic nonchalance. Marcus's clothes, on the other hand, were simply an extension of himself. Tonight a black vest covered a white collarless shirt, the sleeves pushed up. Black slacks finished the ensemble. She'd missed his shoes. All in all, the look said casual, creative and would play well on TV.

Kara wondered if a stylist dressed him.

As she listened to him answer questions in a format similar to the show *Inside the Actor's Studio,* Kara learned a lot about him. And the more she learned, the more she wanted to know.

"We're almost out of time," the moderator said. "Now for the twenty-questions section. You're in the hot seat, Marcus. I'll name twenty things, and you give us the first response that comes to mind."

Kara sat up. If they were going to play Twenty Questions, she had a few. But no one else raised a hand.

Marcus groaned, then sent one of those lazy smiles Kara's way. "I always hate these. It's a good thing I brought my therapist along in case I get in trouble."

Kara just shook her head.

"The first question—plain or peanut?"

Chuckling, he responded, "Peanut. I like variety."

"Coke or Pepsi?"

"Neither," Marcus replied. "I drink more spring water and juice than soda." He leaned back and twisted his head a bit as if sharing a secret with the audience alone. "And she brews a mean cup of green tea."

Kara blushed as all eyes again turned toward her.

"Next question. Sunrise or sunset?"

"Please. I'm a musician. I never see sunrise."

The graduate students laughed, but Kara tilted her head just so, studying him, knowing he wasn't telling the whole truth. She'd seen him at sunrise. From her bedroom window. Wednesday. She'd tried, apparently unsuccessfully, to banish that impression from her memory banks.

As an early riser herself, she'd seen him outside, barefoot and bare chested in his backyard. At first he'd been still, as still as the earth in the hushed moments between night and dawn when the earth itself seems to pause to welcome the gift of the sun's rays. Then, slowly, he'd begun to move in a graceful ballet that she'd recognized as tai chi.

She'd stared out the window at him for a long time. When he finished, he stood there. Just stood. And Kara had wondered if he spent the minutes in prayer. Belatedly feeling as if she were an intruder, she'd let the curtain fall back into place.

Now the clinician in her sat wondering why he preferred to use the musician stereotype. Maybe it wasn't cool to let people know that some musicians were up at dawn toning their bodies and taking pleasure in quiet reflection.

The next few questions from the moderator went along the same lines.

"Blondes, brunettes or redheads?"

Marcus swiveled in his seat until he faced Kara. The cameraman, seeing his focus, shifted direction and zoomed in on her, too. "Definitely brunettes," Marcus said. "With crimped hair and Ph.D.'s."

Kara wanted the floor to open up and swallow her. Had he completely lost his mind?

The moderator cleared his throat. "Well, moving on. If you could change one thing about America, what would it be?"

"Oh, man, you're killing me. This obviously means the easy questions are over."

The audience laughed, and Kara realized—

again—just how comfortable he was on the hot seat. Marcus thought on his feet, a true indication of an intelligent mind behind the facade of laid-back crooner.

"In all seriousness, the number one problem in America today is intolerance. Cultural, racial, economic and religious intolerance. We claim to be a melting pot. But look at eleven o'clock on any Sunday morning. What do you see? The black people go to their churches, the white people to theirs. Where I live, the Korean and Latino communities gather for worship in their own separate places, as well."

"Why is that so bad?" someone in the audience called out. "Religion is one way to boost cultural awareness. I'm biracial and my parents made it their business to make sure I knew both my Italian and my African-American heritage."

Marcus nodded. "And we need more parents like yours. Dr. Kara, what in your professional opinion can people do to promote tolerance?"

Before Kara could formulate an answer, the moderator broke in. "This is supposed to be Twenty Questions for *you,* Mr. Ambrose."

Marcus's mouth quirked in that disarming, enchanting smile. Shrugging to the audience, he said, "My bad, my man."

Later, as the sleek limousine moved through the streets of Wayside, Kara glanced at the man sitting next to her. "Why'd you bounce that question to me?"

"I thought you might enjoy the debate."

"You think I like to fight?"

"Yes."

Her mouth twitched up. "We left Twenty Questions at the college, but I have one. That cameraman, was he one of yours or from the TV stations?''

''Mine. You missed the TV crews.''

''Thank goodness for small favors,'' she muttered.

''You don't like the spotlight.'' The observation sounded almost disappointed.

''I leave that to the people who…'' She paused. ''People who thrive in that environment.''

He stretched his legs out and put his hands behind his head. ''Quite the diplomat, aren't you?''

''You learn quickly when you grow up in a house with six kids and two working parents.''

''I really enjoyed your family Sunday.''

''They enjoyed you, too.''

She'd heard nothing but nonstop praise about ''that nice young man,'' ''that too fine brother'' and ''a celebrity right at my own dining-room table''— the last coming from none other than Gordon Spencer, her unflappable father.

''So how many years are between you and Garrett?''

She glanced at him and smiled. ''Angling for my age, huh?''

''A guy has to take the indirect approach on some things.''

''I was seventeen and mortified when my mother told us she was pregnant. That makes me thirty-one, by the way.'' A small laugh escaped her.

Marcus angled himself so he faced her. ''What?''

''Garrett was their twentieth-anniversary surprise. Ben and Patrice used to torment him by calling him 'Oops.'''

''And big sister Kara was his champion?''

She nodded, remembering the times she'd dried her baby brother's tears.

"I bet you were a terrific big sister. You have a good heart." He reached for her hand and laced his fingers with hers. "You'll make a good mom."

Kara didn't object to the touch. "So, where are we going?"

He didn't call her on the change of subject. "I thought about and rejected the dinner-and-a-movie route."

"In favor of?"

He answered with an enigmatic smile. "You'll see."

"We're going to Portland," she guessed. "The driver just got on the interstate." Feeling a little guilty about changing the subject, she added, "My sister Faye did it the right way."

"Did what the right way?"

"Produced grandchildren. She graduated from Wayside College on a Sunday afternoon and got married the following Saturday. She had two kids exactly one year later, the twins who were running around the house. So far, that's held our parents off. But they keep looking at me and at Ben."

"Feeling a little pressure?"

Kara shrugged and tugged her hand free of his. "Not from them."

The pressure came from internal anxiety. Was she destined to be single her entire life? She had a hard time reconciling herself to that. The singles ministry at Community Christian kept her in fellowship with other singles, but it wasn't a dating service and wasn't supposed to be.

When Haley got married it had really hit home for

Kara that she was thirty and her best prospect was a guy whose electronic gadgets appealed to him more than she did.

"No," she said again to Marcus. "Instead of a husband and babies I brought home degrees, and that's suited them just fine."

If only she could say the same for herself.

She turned up a bright smile and faced him. "What about you? How many brothers and sisters?"

"None."

"You're kidding. You're so lucky."

He cocked his head at her. "Why do you say that?"

"No fighting over the bathroom, the remote control or who gets to sit next to the window. No one borrowing—" she added air quotes to emphasize the word "—your clothes and makeup and shoes. No brother giving your dates the third degree."

"Well, I don't think clothes and makeup would have been an issue."

She hit him. "You know what I mean."

"Yeah."

"Lots of cousins, then?"

He shook his head.

"Really? That must be heaven. You've seen my family—it's huge. And loud. And always in your business."

He'd longed for that type of environment, but he'd grown up in anything but a loving family atmosphere. Taking her hand in his, he lifted it and pressed a kiss onto her hand. Then, still holding her hand, he settled into the soft leather.

The tenderness and the comfortable silence necessitated yet another shift in her thinking. Marcus Ambrose wasn't so bad.

About thirty minutes later the car came to a halt. "Kara?"

She stirred, vaguely disturbed that the comfortable pillow had shifted. Then she shot up, putting a good twenty-four inches of space between them. Color flamed in her face.

"I'm sorry."

He smiled, that slow lazy one that made her insides tumble. "Not a problem, Dr. Kara. Not a problem at all. I enjoyed being your pillow."

To keep from looking at him, she shifted her gaze to the view outside the window. And saw a barren field, peppered spottily with dry brush.

A stab of panic shot through her. She'd gone off with this man and he could do Lord knew what. "Where are we?"

He tapped her on the shoulder and pointed out his window.

Festive lights lit the early-evening sky. Cars and minivans jammed a makeshift lot along the entrance to a winery.

"Oh." Relief washed through her, and she giggled.

"What?"

She shook her head. "Nothing."

"That cute little giggle was about something."

Kara looked at him, then smiled again. "I was, uh, trying to remember if there were any unsolved serial murder cases around here."

"Oh, so now I'm a murderer?"

She reached for his arm, clutched it, willed him to believe her. "No, Marcus. It's just that..." His eyes dipped from hers to her mouth. "See, you can't be too careful. A single woman…"

"Kara?"

He was so close that his breath mingled with hers. "Umm-hmm."

"I'm going to kiss you."

"Uh, okay."

And then he did just that. Slow and easy, a little bit flirty but bold enough to be serious. Kara still held his arm. She leaned willingly into the embrace and deepened the kiss.

"Stop."

"Huh?"

Who'd said what? Kara's befuddled brain didn't seem to operate very well at the moment.

Taking one last kiss, he pushed her away. Shame took this opportunity to introduce itself to Kara. He'd been the one to see reason.

"I…we…" she stuttered. She took a breath, calming her senses, trying to become reconciled to the fact that she'd thrown herself at him and that he'd rejected her. "I'm sorry. I shouldn't have…"

Marcus lifted her chin with his fingers until their gazes met. "I hope you're not about to say you're sorry that things got a little hot and heavy. I'm not. But if we hadn't stopped…" He shrugged. "Well, let's put it this way—I met your father and I don't want him taking a shotgun to my head."

Kara smiled, but it didn't reach her eyes. She'd had no intention of doing anything improper or immoral with him. And he'd just made it perfectly clear that he wasn't really interested in her but wasn't above accepting gifts in the form of a warm and willing woman practically crawling into his lap. But only to an extent.

"Uh-uh," he said when she turned away. "You're thinking too much."

"Maybe we should just..."

He turned her and caught her face between his hands. "If you're going to be thinking about anything at all and analyzing things to the nth degree, analyze this, Dr. Kara."

The kiss he pressed to her mouth sent shock waves ricocheting through her. When he opened the door, Kara sat there stunned, disoriented and most of all overwhelmed.

"Come on," he said. "I don't want you to miss the fireworks."

Miss the fireworks? Couldn't he see? They were going off all around her.

She'd read about this phenomenon. Had heard patients describe it. But never, ever had Kara Lynette Spencer experienced it for herself. Her insides were mushy and she felt the way heroines in romance novels must feel when the hero does something heroic and wonderful.

He held out his hand for her. "Are you coming?"

She reached for her bag. Warmth suffused her when his hand touched her arm, assisting her. Kara tried not to think about it. After stepping out of the car, she smoothed her dress down shakily, and looked up to see him watching her.

He cleared his throat. "Uh, you all right in those shoes?"

Kara looked down. Italian. Imported. A splurge on a business trip to New York. Very expensive. "Yes."

He didn't look convinced, but held his hand out to her again.

Sure that the Lord was going to strike her down for being a wicked woman tonight, Kara put her hand in his.

# *Chapter Eight*

"How did you find this place?"

They'd claimed a cozy spot and stood together watching the multicolored fireworks break in the night sky above. The crowd oohed and aahed at the display. But Kara's attention remained on the man next to her.

Marcus shifted and she found herself in front of him, spooned to him, his arms around her waist.

"I read about it in the newspaper."

"And your assistant set it up?"

He swung his head down. "Nadira? Nah. She's in L.A. I do let my people have some time off."

Kara chewed on that for a bit. Then they simply enjoyed the rest of the fireworks display.

A red, white and blue pyrotechnic burst overhead. The crowd applauded. But Kara's mind was on what they'd done in the car.

"That one was nice."

"Marcus?"

"Umm-hmm?"

She turned in his arms, too late realizing just how close that put them. She stepped back a bit. His arms, though, remained around her. "About what happened in the car…"

"I'm attracted to you, Kara. I'm not going to deny that or pretend that it doesn't exist. But I'm also not going to take advantage of you."

"Why not?"

He chuckled. "Well, isn't this a fine switch in the script."

She shook her head, clarifying her question. "I mean, why are you being such a gentleman? I've been pretty lukewarm toward you."

He let her go. Ice glinted in his eyes. Kara realized, too late, that she'd taken the wrong approach. That he'd taken offense.

"I am a gentleman, *Dr.* Kara." This time she heard no playful affection in the nickname. "You have some sort of preconceived notion about who I am and what I'm supposed to be about. It's wearing thin, Doctor."

"Marcus, I didn't mean…"

"Well, what did you mean?"

Kara carefully chose her words. "All my life I've studied people, human nature. I think that's why I've never been a good candidate for a long-term relationship. Most of the men I know are afraid that I spend my time psychoanalyzing them."

"You do."

Kara frowned, but didn't let his rejoinder stem the flow of what she wanted to tell him. "The night we met, you said I was intense and I denied it."

"Denial is not a river in Egypt," he mumbled.

Either she didn't hear him or she chose to ignore

the comment. ''That was a defense mechanism on my part,'' she said. ''I'm the trained analyst and I guess I didn't like it a lot when the tables were turned.''

''And you're telling me this now, why?''

Well, there was the jackpot question, Kara thought.

''Because I'm confused,'' she finally admitted. ''Where is this going?''

The crowd began to disperse. He shoved his hands into his pockets and started walking toward the area where they'd parked. Falling into step next to him, Kara continued exploring her psyche. ''I'm not like your other women, even though part of me fears I am.''

''My other women?''

Kara looked up at him, surprised at the angry tone. ''What did I say?''

''My other women,'' he repeated, shaking his head. ''For someone who is supposed to be an understanding and open *professional* counselor, you sure have a closed mind.''

He stalked to the car, and Kara ran as best she could in the heels to catch up with him.

The chauffeur waited at the car. Without a word he opened the door for them. Marcus got in, leaving the driver to assist Kara.

''Marcus, I didn't mean—''

He cut her off. ''Save it, Kara. No matter what I do to try to show you that I'm just a regular man you throw some psychoanalytical mumbo jumbo in my face.''

The ride back to Wayside was a silent one. What a difference a few hours could make, Kara thought.

She didn't know how to fill the breach, and Marcus was steamed. In trying to explain herself, she'd only made things worse.

When the car finally pulled in front of her house, she opened the door before the driver came around.

She looked back at Marcus. "I...I'm sorry this didn't work out."

Standing at the curb, she waited for the car to pull into Marcus's driveway next door, but it kept straight down the street. She'd finally gotten what she wanted—Marcus Ambrose out of sight. It would take more than a little time to get this night, their fight...and that kiss out of her mind.

In the limo, Carlton spoke through the intercom. "Where do you want me to go?"

"Just drive."

Kara Spencer had to be the most infuriating woman he'd ever met, Marcus thought. He ran a hand over his face. She was also the most spectacular. He'd never backed down from a challenge, and winning Kara over was definitely proving to be a big one.

He had to ask himself if she made him angry because he'd been unjustly accused...or because what she'd said was true.

One thing he knew for certain. Kara was dead wrong about the electricity between them. He'd put a halt to things in the car because they were about a zipper and a belt buckle away from getting way out of control. Maybe she didn't realize it, but her response to his kisses was anything but lukewarm.

The phone rang early the next morning, its shrill tone aggravating the headache that plagued Kara.

"What did you do to him?" Patrice demanded.

"What time is it?"

"Time for you to tell me why Marcus and Daddy were huddled out back and wouldn't let anybody hear what they were saying."

"Maybe it was a private conversation."

"You're not even funny, Kara. What's going on?"

Rubbing her eyes, Kara shifted to her side. "Seeing as how I'm not Marcus or Daddy, you'll just have to ask them."

"I will."

In a huff, Patrice clicked off. Kara expelled a long breath. Patrice had definitely got all of the Spencer family drama genes. Lifting her head a bit, Kara took a peek at the clock, then let out a shriek.

Ten!

Tossing aside the sheet, she dashed to the bathroom. Her soccer date with Ian was at noon. She'd barely have time to get dressed and to Portland. She finished dressing in record time, and made a quick bowl of oatmeal via the microwave. While the cereal cooked, she listened to the messages on the machine. There were four, all from last night.

"Hi, baby," her mom said on the first one. "Stop over here tomorrow. There's, uh, something I need to, well, I need to talk to you about."

Kara's brow furrowed. What could that be about? She hoped her mother was okay. Ida Spencer wasn't given to mysteries. One thing she'd definitely inherited from her parents—a straightforward, no-nonsense approach to getting the information she needed and laying her cards on the table.

Too bad she'd done just that with Marcus Ambrose.

Maybe if she'd acted more like a bubblehead bimbo or a ditzy lovesick fan she wouldn't be regretting everything she'd said last night. A moment later, when the microwave beeped, Kara amended her thought. If Marcus Ambrose was so thin-skinned that he needed stroking at every turn, she definitely had no business dating him.

"One disastrous date can hardly be construed as dating," she corrected herself.

The answering machine had beeped and moved to the second message. "So if that's all right with you, I'll mark you down."

Kara recognized her pastor's voice, but had missed the beginning of Cliff's message. She reversed the message and groaned at his words. "The church is putting together a benefit concert featuring Marcus Ambrose. Matt is chairing the committee, of course. I'd like you to join him, along with Eunice. She'll be able to set up all announcements. Matt will handle the music and I'd like you to help him with the program. So if that's all right with you, I'll mark you down."

"No, it's not all right with me," Kara said as she sprinkled a bit of brown sugar then a handful of raisins on her oatmeal. The recorder didn't answer back, though, and she spooned up a bit of the cereal. After a beep, the next message began.

"Hello, Kara."

"Ian." She smiled at the way her name sounded with that delicious Scottish burr, warm and sweet, like the instant oatmeal.

"I've a bit of bad news."

Kara frowned. Then she squinted, trying to make

out the discordant noise in the background. Was he in a bar?

"I'm going to have to beg another date with you. No soccer for me today or for a while, I'm afraid. I'm at hospital, you see."

"Hospital?"

The sounds registered then, those emergency-room noises—a television, someone being paged and then a distant ambulance.

"Seems I've broken something. Eh? Oh, they're calling me up. So sorry. I'll call you later."

Kara put the bowl down. She didn't even know what hospital in Portland.

The fourth message began. The display said it had come in at 10:27 p.m. "Hey, sis," Benjamin said. "Got some bad news for you. Your boy broke his leg. He'll be laid up for a while. We were playing rugby on the quad and things got a little rough."

"Rugby?"

"I think he's more upset about breaking a date with you than he is about breaking a leg. You go, girl." Her brother's laughter rang out. "You should hear him moaning. All right, all right, I'm coming," he said to someone in the background. "Check you later, K. Hey, you should go out with that Marcus fellow. He couldn't take his eyes off you Sunday. Big sister got it going on like that."

More laughter and then the phone clattered to the floor or a table.

Suddenly depressed, Kara erased the messages. She finished off the cereal and put the bowl in the sink.

She had the whole day in front of her.

Had anyone asked him why he was at Kara Spencer's parents' house, Marcus would have been hard-pressed for an answer. Maybe the positive vibes from Ida and Gordon made up for the churlish way Kara had treated him the night before. His pride still stung at her insult.

She didn't think he was a gentleman, but he'd show her just what the word meant.

Then again, maybe it was guilt. He'd all but seduced her in his limo.

"Ready?" Gordon asked.

"Yeah."

"On three. One, two, here we go." Grunts and groans came from both men, but they got the large curio into place in the dining room.

"That's going to be just perfect," Ida said from where she stood directing her help. "But maybe a little to the—"

"Ida, honey, we've moved this thing three times. It's going to stay right where it is unless you plan on treating a couple of hernias."

"The piano's next, Gordon."

"Ida!"

She laughed and came over, putting an arm around the waist of each man. "Just messing with you. How about a nice glass of something cold?"

"Water, please." Marcus wiped his brow on the T-shirt that showed sweat marks in several places. Gordon's looked the same. They'd hauled out a buffet and then the new pieces, purchased apparently from a place that didn't deliver.

"One more load and we'll be done," Gordon said. "You all right, young blood?"

Marcus nodded.

"All we have is tap water," Ida told him.

"That's fine," he said.

Gordon gave him a quizzical look. "I thought all you L.A. types drank fancy bottled water."

Well, at least he now knew where Kara got the propensity to make sweeping assumptions. "I have a theory about all those bottles of spring water."

"Yeah," Gordon said. "It all comes from somebody's garden tap in Hoboken, New Jersey."

"For sure you're right."

The three laughed. Ida got Marcus and her husband glasses of water and then the two men headed to the pickup truck Gordon had borrowed to pick up the furniture.

In the truck as they headed into town to drop off the discarded furniture at the women's shelter, Gordon took his eyes off the road to assess the younger man.

"Didn't figure you for a regular Joe."

Marcus sighed. "Folks make a lot of assumptions around here. I put my pants on one leg at a time just like everybody else."

"It's not your pants going *on* that I'm worried about," Gordon said, his tone level.

Marcus met the older man's look as they stopped at a red light. "I'm in Wayside for a month, then I move on to the next city, the next booking."

"And what do you leave behind?"

"Nothing but concert souvenirs."

Gordon, quiet for a moment, measured those words. "For a man like you, I'd reckon you'd leave a trail of broken hearts."

Marcus stared out the window. "Not deliberately."

"A man with four daughters learns what to look out for."

"I imagine he would."

Something about the conversation put Marcus in mind of a Bible story he remembered. How Jacob made a deal with Rachel's father and ended up getting tricked into marrying Leah instead of the woman he wanted. Which daughter did Gordon consider Rachel and which one Leah?

The light turned green and Gordon stepped on the gas. "You don't give much away."

"No need to. There's nothing to confess."

"Ever been married?"

"No."

That earned him a look. "Aren't you about thirty-five?"

"Close. Thirty-three."

"A man's gotta settle down eventually."

Marcus looked out the side window as the bucolic streets of Wayside passed by. It was the sort of place where a man settled down. "Yeah." He finally answered the not-quite-a-question. "A man's got to settle down eventually."

After they dropped off the donation furniture and returned to the house, Ida insisted Marcus stay for dinner. When Kara walked in the front door, the sight that greeted her was Marcus cutting a cherry pie and serving Patrice.

"I've fallen into a nightmare," she muttered.

"Hey, baby. You're just in time for dessert, but I can put a plate together for you and zap it in the microwave."

"No, thanks, Mom. I had a bite already. You said you wanted to see me?"

Ida shot a guilty glance at Marcus, then at Gordon, and nodded. She pushed back from the table. "I think we have some ice cream left. I'll get it."

Marcus's eyes, sharp and assessing, had missed none of the exchange. Nor had Kara's consternation escaped him. He watched as she followed her mother into the kitchen, and he longed to be a fly on the wall in there.

In the kitchen Ida didn't even pretend that she'd come for ice cream. "Did you know Ian broke his leg?"

"Yes. Is that what you wanted to talk to me about?"

Ida peeked over Kara's shoulder. "No. He's a nice boy, a good catch. But Marcus is a better one."

"Mom, please."

"Please, my foot. That boy likes you. If you got your head out of a book for a change you'd see."

"We went out last night." She might as well know, Kara figured.

A broad smile filled Ida's face. "And?"

"And it was an unmitigated disaster."

Ida's expression fell, looking as sorrowful as Kara's own had. "What happened?"

Kara pinched a piece of pot roast from the platter on the island. "Let's just say there wasn't a love connection."

Ida patted her shoulder, then put her arms around her daughter. "Well, maybe Ian is the one."

Kara sighed. Her grace period on producing a husband and kids must have expired.

When she returned to the dining room, no one was there, but music drew her to the family room. Marcus and Patrice sat on the piano bench playing one of his early tunes, a romantic ballad. As Kara listened to the words and watched them together, smiling at each other, enjoying the common interest, she realized any hope she'd hidden in her heart about a possible relationship with Marcus Ambrose was not only unlikely, but improbable.

It was okay to fantasize sometimes. But her own fancy had taken not just a flight but a round-the-world journey. Patrice had what it took to be the flashy partner of an R & B superstar. Kara didn't think she was cut out to be a backstage spouse. Not, of course, that marriage had entered any conversation, but she was thirty-one, so that possibility was always in the back of her mind.

Any second thoughts she had about Marcus would fall into the category of live and learn.

With everyone's attention on the pair at the piano, Kara slipped out of the house.

Kara didn't see Marcus the rest of the week. The vehicles at his house came and went, lights stayed on half the night, but she never actually saw him in person—not even when she got up to peek out the window to watch him at tai chi one day. He'd either finished already or had moved the meditative exercise inside.

However, not seeing Marcus and not hearing about him were two different matters. He was plenty visible in Wayside. Just about every day either the newspaper carried an article or picture about him, or he showed up on her television in a sound bite on the news.

Patrice kept her abreast of things with running updates about the film and music festival. Kara even managed to get to a couple of the film showings—premieres of art house movies made by independent directors and producers. But she steered clear of the screening of Marcus's latest film, *High Alert.*

Neither Matt nor Reverend Baines mentioned another word about the benefit concert planning committee. Kara, who had no intention of bringing it up, came to the only and obvious conclusion: Marcus wanted her off and they'd agreed.

"You're looking kind of droopy around the edges," Haley said.

"I was just thinking the same thing," said Eunice Gallagher, the church secretary.

The three women were in Haley's Sunday-school classroom going over the budget for Community Christian's annual church camp. Donations for the fall event, still several months away, were considerably off target.

Kara shook her head. "Nothing's wrong. I've just been distracted for the last few days. I'm back."

Eunice nudged her. "Distracted by that handsome Mr. Ambrose, I imagine. I can't wait until the concert here."

Kara blew out a shaky breath. "Can we talk about something else?"

Haley and Eunice exchanged a glance. Then Haley picked up a roster. "We had thirty-seven kids last year. The deadline to register is still two weeks away and we already have thirty."

"The last-minute ones usually account for ten to fifteen more," Kara said. "Folks who figure they can swing the registration fee after budgeting for school clothes and supplies."

Eunice did a quick tally on the calculator and

ripped off the tape. "We're gonna be about twenty-two hundred short." She looked at Kara, then spoke to Haley. "We could ask you-know-who for a donation."

"We are not going begging to Marcus Ambrose," Kara declared. "I'll write a check before we do that."

"Two thousand dollars is a lot of money, Kara," Haley pointed out.

"If I get that JUMP grant, we won't have to worry about anything. The camp qualifies as an outreach program. Since fifteen of the kids are coming from the mentoring program, it's a good fit."

"But it'll be six to eight weeks before you hear anything back from them," Haley pointed out.

"And what if we don't get that funding?" Eunice said.

Kara chewed on her bottom lip for a moment. "You're right. Those grants are pretty competitive. We need a solid backup plan."

"Other than you writing a big check," Haley said. "What if we ask Cliff to make a special appeal to the church membership? Maybe we can take pledges."

Kara grinned. "Or ask people to sponsor a kid."

"Hey, that's a terrific idea," Eunice said.

The three women talked about how a sponsorship program might work. Then Eunice sketched a design on the back of the budget analysis. "I can make up some flyers to go in the bulletins."

They huddled over the rough copy and then nodded.

The cordless phone Eunice had brought with her rang. "Are we all done, then?"

Haley and Kara nodded. Eunice picked up the phone and headed to the door with her papers. "Community Christian Church. How may I help you this blessed day?"

When Eunice disappeared, Haley faced Kara. "All right, spill it."

"What?"

"Don't *what* me, Kara. You may not have wanted to talk in front of Eunice, but I know when something's wrong."

"Nothing's wrong," she insisted.

Haley folded her arms and gave Kara one of the looks she reserved for her fourth graders at Wayside Prep.

"He hates me," Kara said under the pressure of that glare.

"Who?"

"Marcus Ambrose."

Kara didn't like admitting it to herself, let alone her best friend, but in the few short days he'd been in Wayside, Marcus had managed to get under her skin. She thought about him constantly. She thought about those two toe-curling, knee-weakening, heart-thumping kisses. First on the terrace the night of the gala, and then the one where she had practically thrown herself at him in the car.

"I seriously doubt if Marcus Ambrose hates you," Haley said.

Kara then caught her friend up on all that had transpired since they'd last talked.

"So he's a little miffed. He'll get over it."

Then Kara told her about Marcus getting cozy with her family.

Haley raised a brow at that. "Maybe he's just being nice. Repaying the kindness. You know your folks, Kara. It's hard to resist them."

"He repaid the kindness when he bought my mother a new dishwasher. This is something else."

"And you, I assume, have a theory?"

Kara nodded. "He's interested in Patrice."

How could she be jealous? Jealous of her own sister.

Again.

Kara blinked back sudden tears. Haley came around the table and put her arms around her friend's shoulders.

"Kara, goodness. What is it?"

Suddenly it all seemed too much to bear. "When is it going to be my turn?"

"What are you talking about?"

"Everybody has somebody," Kara wailed. "Even you." She waved a hand, dismissing the words that could have been taken as a slight. "I didn't mean it that way."

"I know, Kara."

"Faye is younger than I am, and she's married with kids."

"It's not about age," Haley said. "Besides, you're just thirty-one."

But Kara kept right on going. "Ben is getting serious with someone. Erica has a million boyfriends. Even Garrett has a little girlfriend. Now you're having a baby. I'm thirty-one and I'm going to be alone all my life."

She dropped her head onto the table, crying into her arms.

"Kara, that's not true and you know it. Everything

happens in God's own time. The right guy is coming."

"Yeah, and he's apparently walking. From Antarctica or some such place."

"I think you need to stop worrying about this. Look at how things happened with me and Matt. Lord knows I wasn't interested in him. We were at loggerheads from day one." In a protective gesture, she splayed her hand across her stomach. "And now look at us. Married a year with a child on the way."

Kara sniffed again. "You know, when I had that teaching fellowship in Houston, I thought about staying."

"What's Houston got on Wayside?"

Kara sniffled. "Ranches and cowboys and wide open spaces. And did I mention cowboys?"

"I think there's an urban cowboy who triggered all of this."

Kara wiped her eyes and nodded. "Something about him just…" She shook her head, unable to come up with the words. "He just makes me feel so…"

Haley placed a hand on Kara's. "Then he's doing his job, Kara. That's how he's been so successful with his music. Didn't you say that's what he does—and well?"

Kara sat up and blinked. Then she slowly faced her friend.

It was no big surprise that Kara and Haley had wound up as best friends. Their thought processes moved alike in many ways. Kara had already come to the conclusion that Marcus's interest rested solely on the bottom line of his record sales statement.

"Yeah," Kara agreed. "He's figured out the secret

to bottling up all those pheromones. He somehow bottles up that leashed intensity and all that male energy and releases it in just the right dose to millions of adoring female fans.''

Haley looked a bit dismayed. ''Leashed intensity?''

''That's why girls faint at his concerts and do stupid things like throw their underwear on stage.''

Haley's eyes widened and she drew back. ''Please, tell me you're joking.''

Kara cocked her head and an eye at her friend in a gesture that without words clearly conveyed ''I wish.''

''Oh, dear,'' Haley said, suddenly flustered. ''I wonder if Cliff knows about this. We can't have that sort of thing at his concert here. It's supposed to be Christian music. I'm going to talk to Cliff right now.'' She scooped up her papers.

''I'd imagine Marcus would have enough common sense not to sing one of those shimmying songs in church.''

Haley paused at the door. ''I suppose you're right. Matt wouldn't allow anything inappropriate at the church.''

The two women stared at each other, each thinking about Matt's and Haley's battles royal on just that topic.

Haley nodded. ''I'll go catch Cliff.''

When Haley left, Kara glanced at her watch. Time to get back to work. As the associate director at the community resource center, Kara spent much of her time doing paperwork, usually grant applications. The time she spent volunteering in Wayside grounded her to the community and assisted in her efforts to bring in even more resources for people in need.

Right now though the helper felt she needed some help in the coping department.

She blew her nose, looked around the Sunday-school classroom, then gathered her belongings. Sitting around feeling sorry for herself wasn't the way to go about things. Action was.

Her cell phone rang as she headed to her car. "Hello?"

"Hi, Kara. I'm sorry I've been incommunicado for so long. How are you?"

Howard. For some reason, hearing from him didn't cheer her up.

"Just keeping my head above water," she told him as she activated the door.

"Have you eaten?"

Lunch. She could go for lunch. Then she'd head back to get on that grant application. It was almost finished and had to be postmarked the day after tomorrow. "Are you in town or on the highway?"

"Turning onto Main Street right now," he told her.

"I'll meet you at Bouillabaisse." She put the charger on the phone and started her engine.

"Ate there yesterday," Howard said. "How about the inn?"

"That'll do. See you in a bit."

A few minutes later she hugged him and they were seated at a table in the cozy restaurant adjacent to the Wayside Inn. After they ordered, their conversation went the way it usually did—an update on projects at work.

Then Howard said, "I hear you've been seen

around town with Marcus Ambrose. Never listened to his music myself. Different strokes and all that.'' He leaned forward. ''He'll be a great resource for you. Entertainers have a lot of money. Have you decided which project you're going to hit him up for?''

He could have meant it innocently enough, but something in his tone irked Kara—the assumption that a man like Marcus Ambrose couldn't possibly be interested in her or she him unless he supplied a check made out to one of her pet projects.

What did that say about her?

She was about to tell Howard how his seemingly innocent comment came across when an excited buzz swept the room and movement at the dining-room entrance caught her eye.

There stood Marcus with his arm around Patrice.

# Chapter Nine

Marcus immediately spied Kara seated at a table by the window and noticed she didn't lack for male companionship.

No wonder she always looked at him as if he were some sort of lab experiment gone amok. Her tastes apparently ran toward academic types, to put it mildly. First the soccer-playing economist and now this one. The uniform gave him away more than anything else: thin tortoiseshell glasses, khaki pants, blue shirt and loafers. Marcus had seen the look time and again—the folks who ran his Web site operation looked just like him.

He told himself he was being unreasonable, childish even, but he had also noticed that the company she usually kept didn't include African-American men. He'd seen enough brothers in and around town to know they were represented.

But how many men of any race could challenge Kara intellectually in little Wayside, Oregon?

"Ooh, look. There's Kara," Patrice said. "Help me over there."

Marcus nodded at the woman on his arm. "Shouldn't we call a doctor?"

He'd stepped out of his SUV in time to see her take a tumble on the sidewalk in front of the inn. Four-inch heels on cobblestone could do that to a woman. These sisters sure liked their shoes.

"I think I'm all right."

Then why are you clutched around me like I'm life support?

Marcus wanted to voice the question, but refused to lower himself to that acid-tongued level. Instead, the dull headache that had been plaguing him for a week returned in full force. He closed his eyes against the pain stabbing behind his eyes.

"Whoa," Patrice said. "Am I that heavy?"

He hadn't realized he'd swayed. "There's a bench right there," he said, indicating a Victorian sofa at the hostess stand. "Let's get you over there."

The whole place was done up in frills and frou-frou. On another day he might have been amused. He helped Patrice to the seat, then cringed when she loudly called to Kara across the dining room.

Heads turned.

Marcus saw Kara's face flame. Then, with a few murmured words he couldn't make out, she excused herself from her date. A hand he knew to be soft gently touched the other man's hand and shoulder. Marcus frowned. If Kara touched anybody, he wanted it to be...

Stop it, he commanded himself.

If ever there was a woman who didn't want to be bothered with him it was Dr. Kara Spencer. She'd made that abundantly clear. In addition, he realized, she'd been right. Marcus was used to women fawning over him. He hadn't realized he'd come to enjoy it, or even expect it, until Kara showed him just what it felt like to be ignored.

But she hadn't ignored him. Not completely. The kisses they'd shared hadn't been one-sided. Not in the least.

Through her family he'd gotten to know enough about Kara to know she was an old-school kind of woman.

"Patrice. Marcus," the object of his thoughts said. "Did you come for a late lunch?"

"Yes," Patrice said. "Then I had a little mishap outside."

Patrice made it sound as if they'd come together, when in actuality he hadn't even planned to stop here until he saw Patrice stumble and fall.

Marcus noticed a slight tightening at Kara's mouth. Curious, he looked between the two sisters. The resemblance was there, of course. In the eyes, in the bone structure. Kara was obviously older, but not by much. The primary difference was in the way the women carried themselves. Kara confident, assured and always in control, to Patrice's pretty damsel in distress. Given his druthers, Marcus preferred the poised, independent type.

He also liked the compassion in Kara, even when she was…regarding him warily. Could that be a visit from the green-eyed monster? Interesting.

Studying them as the sisters talked, Marcus realized what had just been humming near the surface of his consciousness for a while. He preferred Kara, but not for the obvious reasons. Patrice had been wrapped around him like peppermint on a candy cane. *That* kind of attention he knew too well—and wasn't interested in exploring.

Kara, on the other hand... Well, she was layer upon layer of complex thought, a mysterious creature he wanted to get to know better.

"Does that hurt?" Kara asked, pressing Patrice's ankle.

"A little."

"What about here?"

Patrice winced.

"It might be a sprain."

Kara Spencer was selfless in a society that endorsed and extolled drama queens. What price did Kara pay for that composure and virtue?

His gaze moved toward Kara's lunch companion. The man bent over a piece of paper, not in the least concerned about whatever Kara might be doing. What, if anything, he wondered, did she inspire in him?

"Do you still keep a pair of sneakers in the car?" Patrice asked. "I think I'd better change." The high heels came off.

"It's one-thirty in the afternoon. Why were you in these shoes? My shoes, I might add."

That got Marcus's total attention. He, too, had wondered the same thing. A thin band curved from toe to heel, with another small strap securing the band around the ankle. One of the guys in the band had a very crude name for those kinds of shoes. And they belonged to Kara?

He sent a sidelong glance toward her. Maybe the passion he'd felt in her kiss extended to other areas.

A moment later guilt assailed him. He'd been too long in bad company.

*To be carnally minded is death.* The Scripture from Romans came to him. *But to be spiritually minded is life and peace.*

His physician attributed his frequent headaches to stress. It hadn't occurred to him until just this moment that stress took many forms. Some of which were his own doing.

Maybe it was time to make some changes…and not only in his music.

"Can you walk?"

"I think so."

"Mom should take a look at this. But if you can bear weight, it shouldn't be all that bad."

When Kara looked up at him, Marcus realized the women had been waiting for him to assist Patrice up. She took a tentative step and then another. A grin split her face. "Seems okay."

"I'll go get the sneakers."

Kara headed back to her table to get her car keys. She exchanged a few words with the man, who looked their way and waved, then she wound back through the tables.

Marcus held out his hand. "I'll get them. You can finish your meal with your…date."

Kara looked back at Howard. "Oh, he's—" Then she clamped her mouth shut and dropped the keys into his hand. "Thank you. Patrice, you'll be all right?"

"Umm-hmm. Marcus will see me home, right?"

"Sure," he said smoothly, no expression on his face.

Patrice wrapped her arm around his waist, an action that didn't go unnoticed by Kara or Marcus. "Oh, I almost forgot why I was heading this way. I wanted to get a honey pecan roll."

Kara nodded. "Well, I'll get back to lunch."

While Patrice placed her order, Kara returned to her companion. Marcus watched them, wondering what their relationship might be. Kara leaned down and kissed him on the cheek before taking her seat.

Marcus's gut contracted as if someone had whacked him with a two-by-four.

"What was that for?" Howard asked.

Kara just smiled as she took her seat and carefully placed the cream-colored napkin across her lap. "For being you," she told him. And being in the right place at the right time, she added to herself.

He reached for her hand, and Kara chanced a glance Marcus's way. He was watching!

"Maybe we should make this permanent," Howard said.

Kara's full attention became riveted on Howard and she felt herself tense. "Excuse me?"

"Well, I've been thinking. We're well suited in temperament. We have a pleasant time together. Why not make it a permanent arrangement?"

Not at all sure she was hearing what she thought she was hearing—and afraid she was—Kara shook her head. "What exactly are you saying, Howard?"

He shrugged, as if the proposal carried no great import. "Maybe we should settle down and get married. Everyone expects us to, anyway. We may as well get it over with."

"Aren't you the romantic."

He pursed his lips, and Kara was struck by the contrast between Howard's mouth and Marcus's mouth. Howard had chastely kissed her many times and she'd never felt a tenth of what she felt when Marcus Ambrose simply held her, let alone kissed her.

"We're both pragmatists, Kara. Romance doesn't last forever. Mutual interests and compatibility. Those are the things that sustain a long-term marriage."

That's it. Forget pragmatism. Despite her earlier halfhearted assertions, Kara wanted to be swept off her feet in some overtly romantic way. If a girl wanted romance, Howard Boyd was not the man to supply it. Everything in his world was black and white. It worked or it didn't. Things that didn't work required diligent attention until the problem was corrected. If she insisted on a little romance, he'd approach that just as practically as he would approach bringing a computer system back online. Step-by-step. Blue cord into blue socket, red one there. A few taps on the keyboard and instant operation.

Howard would never drive forty minutes just to see a fireworks display or spend a late Sunday afternoon at the piano singing songs with her family.

"Howard, I don't think—"

He cut her off. "You don't need to answer now," he said. "We can talk later. And do a little planning. Nothing too big. Maybe the country club for a reception?"

Kara bit back panic. "Howard, that isn't…"

Releasing her hand, he picked up his manual. "You know, I think I've figured out why the system at the library keeps going off-line."

Kara stared at him. Pragmatism was one thing— this was something else. How did a man issue a marriage proposal in one breath and then dismiss it in favor of a computer glitch the next? A vision of their anniversaries stretched in front of her. Instead of a diamond anniversary band symbolizing love eternal, which Haley had received from Matt, Howard would probably renew her auto club membership.

She looked toward the door, where Patrice and Marcus still stood. Patrice threw her head back and laughed at something Marcus said.

Kara picked up her fork and ground the tines into the zucchini she hadn't eaten. The appetite she'd had for lunch was gone.

If anyone could relate to the quandary Marcus found himself in, it was Matt Brandon-Dumaine. The music director at Community Christian Church had spent a good deal of his early life in the public spotlight and knew the perils and temptations associated with being a single man on the road.

They were in the large auditorium at the college blocking up the benefit concert. Normally one of his staff would have handled this, but Marcus wanted the time to talk to Matt.

"How much do you know about Kara Spencer?"

Matt shrugged. "She's good people. My wife's best friend." Matt smiled. "They both, however, suffer from major cases of do-good-itis."

Marcus chuckled. "And that would be?"

"When I met Haley she was on, like, eighty boards and sixty volunteer committees. Kara's the same way."

Understanding the exaggeration, Marcus merely nodded. "And now?"

Matt smiled. "She's still active in the community,

but now Haley has other things to focus on. We're expecting our first child."

Marcus slapped him on the back. "Congratulations."

"We're pretty excited about it. But you didn't ask me about Haley. You're interested in Kara?"

"I'm interested in a lot of things," Marcus hedged. He sat down on the stool in front of the grand piano on the stage, opened the lid and played a few bars of an up-tempo melody, then frowned. "This has to be tuned before we can use it."

"I'll see to it. And to answer the question you haven't asked, yeah, Kara's pretty special. I'd hate to see her get hurt. Especially by somebody just passing through town."

First her father, now Matt. He bet Kara had no idea how many champions she had.

"Maybe I'm not passing through."

Matt shrugged. "I was the same way. Wayside kind of grows on you."

"What are some of Kara's pet projects?"

Matt thought about it for a moment. "She works over at the resource center and volunteers with the senior citizen home next door. She and Haley are both on the Founder's Day Celebration committee. They'll be ramping up for that soon. And then there's the historical society and all the stuff they do. But Kara really gets into building things."

"Like what?"

"Mostly houses and sheds in East Wayside."

"I think I drove through there. Homeless people, folks hanging around on the street corners?"

"That would be it. Our little pocket of poverty.

Kara's determined to single-handedly change the face of East Wayside."

"How so?"

"Mostly through the grants she writes. She gets money from private foundations, the state, the feds. Anybody who will cough up any cash that she can then funnel to assorted community organizations and projects."

Marcus tugged on his collar, then pulled the lid back on the piano. "Grants, you say?"

Matt nodded. "She's been working on one for the JUMP group. I know because I wrote a letter of reference for it. She's probably mailed it off. I think the deadline is today."

Tomorrow, Marcus corrected, but he didn't say anything to Matt. They finished up their stage blocking and then parted company, Marcus excusing himself after pulling out his cell to deal with a complication he hadn't bargained on.

Back at the house he sat with Nadira in the living room. "She can't find out I'm connected to the foundation."

"All right, Marcus. But it's going to look a little odd when…"

"She can't find out."

The assistant nodded.

"I have a project for you."

She pulled out her PDA and stylus. The instrument hovered over the display ready to take notes.

"Find out the name of a building project in town, something similar to Habitat for Humanity, if not that program. I want to know the next time and place they're working. And get me a hard hat or something."

Nadira raised a brow. "You're going to build a house?"

"Is that so odd?"

"Seeing as how you're allergic to wood chips and hay and the pounding is likely to bring on a headache, I'd say yeah."

"Well, stop thinking so much."

She grinned and stood up. "Must be love."

"Hey…" he called, but she was already headed out the door.

*Love?*

Couldn't be. Marcus had never been in love before. At least, not the kind of love that promised vows and commitments and oaths of till death do us part.

But what was really so wrong with that kind of holy commitment—with the right woman? Matt Brandon-Dumaine looked happy. Very happy.

Marcus knew he shouldn't compare his life and circumstances to others. Still lost in thought, he went to the electric piano and played around for a bit, before his hands settled into a song he remembered from his youth, from the days when the woman he called his grandmother took him to church every Sunday, Wednesday and Friday night. Marcus had never lost his faith. He'd just let it get buried— smothered was more like it—under the demands of running a production company, supervising the charitable foundation he operated in secret and managing the lives and careers of a twenty-five-person staff. In between all of that, he found time to write music, get to the studio to record it, act in a film or two and maintain a national touring schedule.

His head started pounding.

''Nadira!''

She came back, with a glass of water and two tablets in her palm. ''You need a vacation, Marcus.''

''How do you do that?''

''Do what?''

''Read my mind the way you do.''

She smiled, that Cheshire-cat look that did nothing to relieve his suspicions that his ever-efficient assistant had him under twenty-four-hour stealth surveillance.

''If I told you all my secrets, you wouldn't pay me as much as you do.''

He laughed. ''Ain't that the truth.'' He took the pain relievers and washed them down with the water.

''Is that from the tap?''

''No, it's the water we brought up from L.A.''

''Hmm.'' He made a note to ask Ida Spencer what kind of water she used. It had been perfect at her house, like cool spring water from a clean mountain stream. And he hadn't had a single headache on the days he spent over there. Or with Kara.

''You know,'' she said, ''these headaches aren't going to go away until you get some R and R.''

''And that diagnosis is from your extensive medical training?''

''It's from common sense. I'm worried about you, Marcus. You act like you're not human sometimes. You've been burning the candle at both ends and from the middle for nine straight months. You're exhausted and don't even know it.''

He held out his hand. ''Messages.''

Nadira sighed.

Since he refused to get attached to a PDA, she had to give him his messages the old-fashioned way.

From a pocket she pulled out several slips of paper and gave him the summary as she flipped through them.

"Two from Jerry, who wants to know when you can come in to shoot the next album cover. One from your agent. There's a script he wants you to read, another action-adventure film. But you need to hurry, because a couple of other people are also on the shortlist."

Marcus sat with his eyes closed, his head thrown back. "Are you listening?" Nadira asked.

"I heard you. Jerry's about to have an aneurysm and Quentin wants another fat paycheck. Go on."

On a sigh, Nadira continued. "Two from the music and film festival coordinator at the college. She says the master class went so well they want a repeat. And she wanted to remind you about the reception at the mayor's house tomorrow night. The local columnist, Cyril Abercrombie, wants an exclusive interview. Six from fans who've managed to get this number. And one from somebody named Ida inviting you to dinner after church Sunday."

He sat up. "Which one's Ida's?" He could use some time at that house. Particularly with these headaches.

She held it up. He plucked the message from her hands.

"Who's Ida? I thought you were interested in Kara."

Ignoring the rest of the messages, including the urgent ones from his agent and the record-company rep, he pulled out his cell phone. "Confirm for two attendees at the mayor's," he said as he punched in the Spencer number. "And change the landline phone numbers. All of them. I'll give you a list of need-to-know people.''

Nadira stood there holding the other slips of paper when he showed no sign of taking them. ''What about these? You really need to make a decision about…''

He held up a finger. Nadira stopped talking.

''Hi, Mom Spencer. I got your message.''

With a wave of his hand he signaled for some privacy. On another long-suffering sigh, Nadira left the remaining messages within reach on the piano.

As she exited, she heard, ''I'd love to come to dinner.''

Kara wasn't surprised to often see Marcus at the dinner table or in the kitchen when she stopped by her parents' house. For just that reason she'd cut her visits way back, relying instead on the phone. She also had the reports from her spies, namely Erica and Garrett. According to her youngest brother and sister, Marcus had become something of a regular at the Spencer house. Patrice spent most of each day in a giddy fog, playing Marcus's CDs over and over until Gordon called for a twenty-four-hour moratorium. And Erica's friends had taken to stopping by at all hours of the day and night in the hope of getting to see Marcus.

In other words, the Spencer house had turned into even more of a three-ring circus than usual. Of course, under *this* big top Marcus played the role of ringmaster, head clown and the main event.

Counting the days until he was out of Wayside, and therefore out of her life, Kara was looking forward to releasing a lot of pent-up energy and frustration at the new home site in East Wayside. A group of volunteers would get the frame up and begin on the outer walls today. They planned to work through the day and all of tomorrow to get the house ready for its occupants, a family of four that had been on the waiting list for more than a year.

Kara donned work boots and jeans, a T-shirt and covered her hair with a scarf tied at the back. "There's no ailment that a little hard work won't cure."

The atmosphere was festive at the work site. The crew had done this together several times before and everyone quickly got into the groove of the building project. They'd been working for about three hours when at 11:20 a limousine, two television satellite trucks and three black SUVs pulled in front of the house in progress.

"Looks like we have company," the foreman called out. "Keep working. I'll see what's up."

Kara glowered in the general direction of Marcus's entourage as they climbed out of the vehicles. The man himself was dressed as if he'd come to work. Disbelief tempered her glower until one of the TV camera operators sidled in front of him. Then she spotted Belinda Barbara, the Portland TV anchor, edging her way over to what would eventually be a modified wraparound porch.

"Great," Kara muttered. "Just great." As usual, the regional celebrity looked crisp and fresh, ready to strut down a runway, while Kara, on the other hand, had grit in her mouth, calluses on her hands and sawdust in her hair.

"Well, hello again. Dr. Kara, isn't it?"

Wiping her mouth on her sleeve, Kara nodded. "Dr. Spencer. How are you?"

"How about a shot over here, Sonny," the television personality said, ignoring Kara's greeting. "I can do the stand-up right here and that'll give you plenty of space to pan out for a wide shot."

An assistant trotted back to the van for equipment, while Belinda made a beeline for Marcus.

"It isn't every day that a celebrity such as you takes up a cause such as this one," she said.

Marcus, in full charm mode, smiled for her and said something Kara couldn't quite make out. She put down the power saw she'd been using and secured the safety as she edged closer to the chitchat.

"I want to do my part," she heard Marcus say.

She snorted.

Belinda turned around. "What was that, Dr. Kara?"

"Dr. Spencer," Kara said, hoping she didn't sound as irritated as she felt. He had some nerve showing up here, pretending that he was part of this project. "Isn't today the day you're supposed to be hosting the showing of your films?" she asked Marcus.

"I didn't realize you kept track of my schedule."

Kara's eyes narrowed at the taunt.

Belinda chortled. "I see the two of you still haven't resolved your differences. But," she said with a wave that encompassed the construction site, "at least you're hard at work on that challenge. Is this your so-called 'real world,' Dr. Kara?"

"There was no challenge," Kara said.

"I'm here seeing to my end of it," Marcus said over her.

Kara's eyes widened. What game was he playing now?

But true to his word, Marcus worked. After taking direction from the project foreman and donning a white face mask like the ones another pop star wore all the time, he pulled his share of the load. Even after the television crews packed up their cables and cameras and microphones, even after Kara conked out. The only break had been for a fast boxed lunch of roast beef sandwiches, an apple and a couple of oatmeal cookies.

"You surprise me," Kara said, wiping her brow with a red handkerchief.

It had been a long, productive day. Tired in places she hadn't expected she could be tired, she plopped onto the front porch step and leaned on a large white cooler.

"Because I'm not the spoiled slacker you think I am?"

She quirked her head. "As a matter of fact, yeah."

He propped a foot on the bottom step, a hammer dangling from his hand. "Why don't you give me a chance?"

"A chance to what?" Break my heart? she added to herself.

"To break that stereotype you've been walking around with."

Twisting around, Kara reached into the cooler for a bottle of water. She handed a dripping one to Marcus. After quenching her own thirst, she screwed the cap back on her bottle.

"We're from different worlds," she told him.

"I'm a man, Kara. I put my pants on just like everybody else."

She shook her head. "That's not what I mean. We have different value systems. I'm a Christian, Marcus. I can't condone the things you sing about, the images I see on the music videos supporting your songs. For you it's all about a good time, carnal pleasures. I'm about kingdom work, making a difference on this earth."

"And you think I don't share those values?"

She shrugged. "With the exception of today, which was done for the TV people, may I just point out, I've never seen any evidence of any higher calling on your part."

He pursed his lips for a moment, then took another long drink of water. "There's a lot more to what I do besides what you see."

"Okay."

"Okay?"

Kara held her hands up in surrender. "What do you want me to say, Marcus? I haven't seen any evidence."

"Isn't that the definition of faith? The evidence of things not seen."

Her gaze met his and her eyes narrowed. "Where did you say you went to school?"

"You asked me that before."

"And as I recall, you never gave me a straight answer."

"Why does it matter? Are you one of those academic snobs who'll only associate with people from the right colleges, people who have the right degrees?"

"That's not fair."

"Neither is your characterization of me as a playboy with nothing on his mind but bump and grind."

Kara stood up. "Then why do you sing the music you sing?"

He walked away.

She flung her hands out wide. "This is how you have a fight? You just leave?"

Without a word to her, he opened the door on his SUV, leaned in and then slammed the door before returning to her. He stood so close that Kara again realized just how intimidating a physical presence he could be.

"My music is about more than what you've obviously listened to," he said. He offered her a cassette tape.

She stared at it as if the thing had been dipped in anthrax. "What's that?"

"It's a rough," he said. "Six of the songs on a project I'm working on. Listen to them."

"I don't want to."

He smiled then, and Kara realized the trap she'd laid for herself. "Because you'll see just how wrong you've been?"

She snatched the tape from him. "Because I don't want to be offended by music that should carry an R or X rating."

But Marcus was already headed back to his truck. He started the engine, revved it and called out to her. "The mayor has a reception at six-thirty tomorrow. I'll pick you up at six-fifteen."

"Of all the nerve," Kara sputtered.

But she grumbled to an empty lot.

She wanted a shower like crazy, but she wanted to hear what he had on that tape even more. Kara made a stop to buy a recorder that had a tape function. Her car and the sound system in her house supported only CDs.

She hustled into the house, dropped the bag and the tape on the counter and made herself get cleaned up first. After washing away the dust and grime of the day, she brewed a cup of tea, stuck batteries in the tape player and listened to the point he wanted to make.

The first song on the cassette was the one Patrice had read at dinner. What she heard was rough—it was just Marcus alone and a piano. No backup singers, no drums or violins or synthesizers. The unpolished music was pure praise.

''I will sing praises to You, the One on high. Your adoration has sustained me, made me whole and sublime.''

The handwritten label said the song was titled ''Adoration.''

The next one had no lyrics. Marcus—she assumed it was him—simply played the piano. Kara sang along, the words to ''All to Jesus'' bubbling up from within her.

When it ended, she rewound and listened again.

She glanced out the window at the house next door. Two of the SUVs were there. Marcus apparently hadn't gotten back. As she dropped the curtain back into place, she saw three people head out his back door, the savvy assistant Nadira and two men. They climbed into the trucks and backed out of the drive.

The rest of the music on the tape consisted of two hymns, one with a jazzy arrangement, and two pieces that she'd never heard before, possibly original tunes.

But the bottom line came through loud and clear—

if this truly was his next project, Marcus Ambrose's music was shifting to a different audience. His fan base of screaming, panting women wouldn't like this at all.

But Kara Spencer loved it.

# Chapter Ten

She listened to the entire cassette tape again as she prepared and ate a light dinner of pasta salad. Sitting in the sunroom, she saw when the SUV pulled in.

Without thinking about the consequences, she got up, went outside and waited for him to get out of the truck.

"Marcus?"

He turned.

"Would you like to come over for a cup of tea?"

He knew it probably wasn't a good idea, but he pocketed his keys and crossed the yard.

"I've been meaning to come over to borrow that cup of sugar," he said. "I guess now's a good time to collect it."

She opened the door wide, letting him pass. When he brushed against her, he heard her quick intake of breath.

No, it wasn't a good idea for him to be this close to temptation.

She led him through the sunroom and to the

kitchen. "I made a lemon chiffon cake. Would you like a piece?"

Her kitchen bore no resemblance to her mother's. At Ida's, dark cabinets, sunny curtains and jammed countertops along with a refrigerator plastered with memos about doctor appointments, photos of ball games and piano recitals, plus aged artwork pegged Mrs. Spencer's domain as the family headquarters.

He liked the blue-and-white stuff, but Kara's kitchen glistened with the seldom-used look of a television set. Shiny pots, carefully arranged green plants and stainless steel appliances sparkled like new. The only hint that any cooking actually happened in the space was a huge collection of cookbooks and spices.

"You can cook?"

She chuckled. "Ida passed all those cooking genes my way. Why does that surprise you?"

He shrugged as he snagged a chair and straddled it. "You don't seem like the type to spend a lot of time chained to a stove."

"That's because I don't. Much like an organized mind, an organized kitchen can produce some pretty remarkable results."

She placed a dessert plate in front of him with a generous piece of cake, then she held out a fork. "Try it. I dare you."

He took the fork, cut off a piece of the cake and did a taste test. A moment later he moaned.

"Marry me. Please. Right now."

Kara laughed out loud and turned to pull down a couple of mugs. She cut a much smaller piece for herself. After the tea steeped, she joined him at the table.

He finished off the cake in short order and looked

up for more. Kara pushed the cake plate and knife his way.

"I owe you an apology," she said. "You were right—"

"Stop the presses," he called out. "We have a front page story here."

"You're not being very gracious about this."

He winked at her, then wolfed down more of the lemon chiffon cake.

Kara reached for his hand. "I'm serious, Marcus. I did rush to judgment, and that was wrong."

"What changed your mind?"

"You did, really. Your music."

"So you listened to the tape."

She nodded. "That's really a project in the works?"

"I need about five more pieces for it. I don't quite have the right mix yet. There's still a little time to work things out." The messages he'd yet to answer from L.A. came to mind. He really needed to fly down there and put out a few fires. Maybe he didn't have as much time as he claimed. He wouldn't stress about it. The right music always came together. Besides, his manager was going to have a stroke about a gospel album anyway.

"There are some contest finalists, songwriters, I'm supposed to meet with. I may get lucky with one of them."

"Have you talked to Matt Brandon-Dumaine?"

"As a matter of fact, I have. He's already signed on to do a duet with me."

"That's great. I think he's missed that sort of thing." Kara winced. "That didn't come out quite right."

Marcus smiled, cutting her some slack. "I knew what you meant."

They seemed to run out of things to say. He watched as she twirled her fork in her fingers.

"Do you play?"

"Play what?"

He nodded toward her hands. "Piano."

Smiling, she put the fork down. "Not as well as I could."

An intriguing choice of words, he thought. But he let it go. The last thing he wanted was her thinking along any track that would lead to a resumption of the cold war between them.

"So," Kara said, "what do you think of Wayside?"

"I think I landed right in the middle of Mayberry."

"You're making fun."

"Actually, no," he said. "Have you ever been to L.A.?"

She nodded. "For a psychologists' conference. But I didn't see much beyond the hotel and the airport."

"L.A. is crazy. Sometimes you just can't breathe. And I mean that literally and figuratively. I have a place away from all of the hustle. After coming to Wayside, I wish I could pick up that house and plop it right here."

"Wayside isn't Utopia."

"Could have fooled me."

He leaned back, took a sip of his tea.

"This is a great blend. Where'd you find it?"

"A tea shop in Portland. I'll give you the address," she said.

In addition to baking like Betty Crocker, the woman knew the intricacies involved in making a great pot of tea. He held the cup up. "Not a soul on my staff can make a decent pot. You sure you won't marry me?"

She looked away, but smiled. "Stop playing."

Something shifted in Marcus and he put the cup down. He'd issued the proposal, twice now, in jest. But the idea of being married to Kara Spencer didn't give him the heebie-jeebies and he didn't spontaneously burst out in hives. As a matter of fact, he rather liked the notion. A lot.

What might her answer be if he asked in earnest?

"Have you had an official tour of Wayside?"

"Official—you mean like the mayor showing me around?" He shook his head. "I've seen Main Street." He smiled. "It's quaint. Cute with all the little shops, the ice cream parlor. I'm telling you, if Hollywood ever finds this place, you guys are gonna be swamped."

"It won't happen," Kara said. "We get too much rain."

"It hasn't rained since I've been here. Did you order that up special for me?"

"You are a flirt, aren't you?"

"Not really."

She raised an eyebrow at that. "From everything I've seen…" He placed his hand on hers and her words fell off.

"I'm comfortable with you, Kara. I enjoy your wit, your humor and even the biting sarcasm you let loose every now and then."

"I am not sarcastic."

He grinned. "Then I must bring out the worst in you."

He could see she was getting flustered, so he deliberately steered the conversation back to safe territory. "Would you show me your town?"

"I beg your pardon?"

"You said there's more to Wayside than its idyllic downtown. Show me."

"Idyllic. Where did—"

He cut off the question, knowing what she was about to ask. Again.

His official bio gave no hint, and Marcus didn't flaunt the information, but he held not only an undergrad degree in music education, but two master's degrees, as well. One in business administration and the other, a master's degree in biblical literature with an emphasis on the Psalms.

His studies had served him well throughout his career. Kara Spencer didn't realize it, but she was an academic snob—at least when it came to her personal associations. That guy she'd been eating lunch with—the one she'd kissed—probably had Ph.D.'s in chemistry and quantum physics from MIT.

With an effort he tucked the jealousy away. "I just have another week here. I'd hate to miss the essence of the town."

Kara took their empty plates and put them in the dishwasher. "I wouldn't go so far as to say Wayside has an essence."

"Then tell me about you," he said.

Kara whirled around. "Me? You already know about me."

He got up, joined her in the kitchen. "Not really. You're a psychologist. You bake a mean lemon chiffon cake. You have a large, open family. You're my next-door neighbor. There's more to the woman than that.''

Kara tucked a strand of hair behind her ear and busied herself with a nonexistent cleanup. ''You're crowding me.''

Even though he knew he wasn't violating her personal space, he stepped back. Dealing with Kara was a lot like handling eggshells. ''I make you nervous.''

''Yes. I mean no.''

Smiling, he did crowd her then by stepping close and stilling the hands that wiped down the counter. ''I'm not the bogeyman, Kara. I'm just a guy who earns a living by singing music. I'm in town, in Wayside, for a few weeks, and then I'm gone.''

''Then why…''

''You're the most interesting person I've met since I've been here. I'd like to get to know you a little better. That doesn't mean I'm about to jump your bones.''

''Marcus!''

''Good Christian girls don't do that sort of thing?''

''You're making fun of my beliefs.''

He placed one hand over his heart and held hers in the other. ''No, Kara. I'm telling you that despite the conclusions you've come to about me, I share your beliefs.'' He pressed a kiss to her hand and had the pleasure of watching her eyes widen.

Then, stepping away, he indicated the cassette player on the counter. ''That tape you listened to, that's the Marcus that nobody knows. Nobody except you. Thanks for dessert and tea.''

He let himself out the back door and headed across the path to his own house.

Kara didn't know what to make of their conversation, of his confession, or of her conflicting emotions. Marcus Ambrose lived one way and talked another. Or did he?

She'd assumed a lot about how he lived. But did she really know? Did she really know *him?* She'd always been taught, had always believed that what you see is what you get. What if she'd deliberately avoided seeing the truth about Marcus? Her entire impression of him had been built on not the man, but the idol—and even that through Patrice's eyes, instead of her own.

Before he'd arrived in Wayside, Marcus Ambrose hadn't been a man, he'd been a myth. A poster on the wall. A voice coming through the radio.

Now that she'd spent a little time with him, he'd become so much more. He was a person. And you had relationships with people, not with myths and idols.

After a glance at the cake on the table she made up her mind. She cut and wrapped two large slices and quickly made her way across the path to his back door.

"Did I leave something?" he asked.

"Just this." She held up the peace offering. "What are you doing tomorrow? I can give you the grand tour of Wayside."

He smiled. "I'd like that."


They stood in front of the building known as the Train Depot. The weather, sunny and warm with not even a puff of white cloud marring the sky, cooperated today as if Mother Nature didn't want anything to taint Kara and Marcus's walking and driving tour of Wayside. Kara gave him a bit of the town's history at the gazebo, noting in particular the cherry trees planted at each directional corner.

"Haley is the serious historian. I'm a member of the historical society, but I mostly write grants for state and federal funds."

He glanced at her. "Kara, about those grants…"

"I know," she said, cutting him off with a smile. "Haley tells me all the time that I can find money where none exists. Preparing a good grant proposal is like working a logic puzzle. There are certain things, buzz words and phrases if you will, that hook a committee."

"Oh, really."

Kara nodded. "I just finished an application for a JUMP grant. JUMP is a foundation designed to get kids interested in the arts and off the streets. Are you familiar with it?"

"Uh, vaguely."

"I'm really excited. I think we have a really good shot at landing one this year. But the competition is pretty keen."

Tell me about it, Marcus thought. He'd already winnowed the early arrivals to a list of five. Those project requests would ultimately be pitted against the best of the ones that came in before the deadline. Kara's application packet would probably arrive in the mail pouch from L.A. in a day or two.

She didn't know it, but he'd given her project a green light the moment he'd found out she was applying.

"Kara, there's something you—"

"Look there," Kara said, pointing to a miniature display in the window of the Train Depot. "I just love the window displays they do here. That's our founder, Edwin Cherry, and his wife, Sheridan. They headed west from Missouri following the Lewis and Clark expeditions, but settled here, opened a trading post and made a fortune. The way I find funding, maybe I would have been a good gold prospector during the rush.''

''I don't think women did that.''

''Women pulled their fair share and more in settling the West. They had mining claims right alongside the men.''

Smiling, he laced his hands behind his back. ''I stand corrected, then.''

Kara eyed him sidelong, but if she'd sensed a touch of condescension in his tone, he hid it well. More than anything, he'd seemed truly interested as she rattled off Wayside history, population and economic figures that would have had the mayor and chamber president beaming. ''Before we finish today, you'll have to get a piece of cherry pie. It's what we're known for in the region.''

''I'll look forward to it.''

This time she did look at him. She hadn't been mistaken about his tone. His voice sounded husky…and hungry? Maybe it was talk of pie. But the look in his eyes belied that.

Keenly aware of his scrutiny, Kara licked her lips. He leaned forward, and she stopped breathing for a moment. Was he really going to kiss her right out here on the street? In front of God and everybody?

With a hand placed at her collar, she cleared her throat. ''I…'' She glanced around. ''Let's move on.''

She didn't want to read his expression for fear that

her own would match his. Twice now Marcus Ambrose had kissed her, and if the truth were known—
not that she had *any* intention of letting him know—
she wanted to kiss him, too.

"If this is the train depot, where are the tracks? I
don't think I've seen any anywhere."

Kara laughed, the air between them light and easy
again. "Quite observant of you, Mr. Ambrose. The
spot where this building stands marks the boundary
of the original town settled by our founders. But the
railroad never passed through Wayside."

He looked at the building. Its weathered facade
emitted an air of bygone grandeur as if the station,
a lowly cousin to its architecturally grander Union
Station relatives, still knew how to maintain its dignity.

"Then why do you have a train depot?"

Kara smiled and took his hand. "Come on in. I'll
show you."

Inside the depot elaborate model trains chugged
around miniature villages and towns. The entire place
paid homage to the railroad.

"You should see it at Christmas," Kara said.
"Fabulous."

It might be nice to spend Christmas in a place like
Wayside. As he'd grown up, the holiday had meant
little to him, except the one year he'd spent it with
Mrs. Washington, his "grandmother." Christmas
generally depressed him, so each year he threw a big
party for his people and their families, then volunteered to entertain the military troops overseas or
dish up meals at a mission—anything to avoid being
alone.

Shaking off the melancholy track of his thoughts,

he greeted the curator, who addressed Kara by name and welcomed them to the Train Depot.

Following their tour, Marcus bought matching conductor hats for them. He stuck Kara's on her head at a jaunty angle. "All aboard!"

Kara just shook her head at his antics.

They said their farewells and he took her hand.

"Where to next?" he asked after seeing her into the car and walking around to the passenger side.

"If you like, I'll show you where Edwin and Sheridan are buried."

"It's your tour."

They drove for about five minutes. Then Kara stopped at a park lined with what Marcus had come to recognize as cherry trees.

"This is the oldest cemetery in town," Kara said. "Most of the first families are buried here." When he didn't move, she glanced over at him. "Are you okay with this? I know some people don't like cemeteries. We don't have to go in."

"No, I want to. I actually enjoy looking at old gravestones."

Kara smiled. "So do I. I get such a sense of history and perspective. You know, like I'm here to do my work for my season, and then I'll rest for a season under a green tree."

"He restoreth my soul." Marcus murmured. He stared at her for a moment, then slowly nodded. "That's exactly it."

Together they walked along the rows, pausing now and then to read an epitaph. While the headstones and markers clearly identified the place as a cemetery, the town had done a remarkable job of making the atmosphere anything but morose.

''The historical society has a project going trying to identify the unreadable stones in one of the older sections.''

With a wicked smile he said, ''And you wrote the grant for the exhumations?''

Instead of being insulted, Kara laughed out loud. ''My skills don't extend quite that far.''

Silent for a while, they each paid silent tribute to those who had gone on. Then Kara said, ''I like coming here sometimes just to think, to put things in perspective. Is that why you bought that Bible in Yesterday's Treasures?''

She'd thought it odd that he'd lingered in the antique shop, one of their many stops. He'd looked at an old family Bible for a long time, then had gone to talk with the owner about its provenance. Before they'd left, Marcus had had the Bible and a small journal wrapped and packaged to take home.

''I like old things that have belonged to other people.''

''Why?''

Marcus shrugged. ''I get a sense of belonging, of carrying on a tradition.''

Something else they had in common.

Kara processed that information, and another piece of the puzzle that was Marcus Ambrose slid into place. She didn't know any men who liked walking in cemeteries or who would admit to buying an old journal and a family Bible for sentimentality's sake.

Surreptitiously she studied Marcus as he read the stones. Slowly she put the pieces of the puzzle together. Then it all clicked. ''My family,'' she said, making the final connection.

He glanced at her. ''What about them?''

''You weren't trying to crowd my space. You wanted to belong.''

Releasing her hand, he stepped away. ''Don't psychoanalyze me, Kara.''

''It's what I do,'' she said. ''And it explains some things.''

''I'm not a lab experiment for you to dissect.''

She reached for his hand, then came around to face him. ''I know. And I hope you don't really feel that way. This is the way my mind works. Tell me, Marcus.''

He looked over her head at the horizon, not seeing the gravestones and markers dotting the green fields of the cemetery.

With a gentle hand she touched his face, drawing his gaze to hers. ''Tell me. Please. I want to understand.''

''There's nothing to understand,'' he said. ''It's pretty simple. I'm a loner.''

''No, you're not.''

He sighed and closed his eyes. ''I grew up in an orphanage,'' he said. ''Nobody wanted to adopt a little black boy with behavior problems.'' He shrugged. ''I always acted out. After being shunted from foster home to foster home, I figured I might as well get the rejection part over with. By rejecting them, I got to control the situation. I could reject them before they kicked me out and sent me back to the home.''

Kara had heard similar stories from her patients but his made her heart tighten painfully. ''And you always wanted a big family?''

He nodded, but the gesture seemed forced out of him. "One of the aides at the home, Sarah Washington, used to take me to church with her. I loved the songs we sang there, and the way the preacher called everyone a family, all of us God's children. I liked to pretend that Mrs. Washington was my grandmother. And I made up stories about how the only reason I didn't live with her and her family was because she was too old to care for me."

Kara's heart went out to the little boy who grew up feeling unloved and unwanted, and to the man who still felt haunted by that early experience.

"Your staff?" she asked. "That's why you have such a large entourage. They're your surrogate family."

He nodded again. "I'm really good at making up excuses for why I can't be in a house or hotel suite alone. They probably don't even realize it." He glanced at her. "You probably think I'm crazy. Maybe it's from all those years in the home. There were always people around. All the time." He shrugged. "I guess I got used to it."

Kara slipped her hand in his. "No, I don't. Think you're crazy," she added.

But something else he'd said sparked speculation within her. The music. As a sexy R & B star, singing love songs with suggestive lyrics, he'd found a way to get the adulation and confirmation he hadn't had as a child. The counselor in Kara wanted to explore that avenue of thought, but she didn't want to alienate him, not now when she found herself drawn to him in this way.

"Whatever happened to Sarah Washington?"

He grinned. "She's eighty-eight and manages the fan clubs at my office in L.A."

At a little bakery shop on Main Street, they ate cherry pie and then Kara dropped Marcus off at Community Christian Church, where the first practice for the concert would be held. Not surprisingly, the parking lot overflowed with cars from church members who, wanting to take part in the concert with a celebrity, had suddenly remembered they sang in one of the choirs.

"I've enjoyed the day," Marcus said.

"Me, too. You've been good company."

He chuckled. "That almost sounds like a concession."

"I thought we weren't going to fight."

He leaned over, pressed a kiss to her forehead. "We're not. Thanks, Dr. Kara."

He opened his door and Kara started the car. "I know you sing. I saw that family video. You're not coming in?"

She shook her head. "No, I…" I need to go home and sort out all the confusing things I'm feeling about you. "I have something to do," she told him.

He smiled, and Kara's insides did that meltdown thing again, a frequent occurrence when Marcus was around.

She powered the window down when he came around to her side of the car. "I really enjoyed today," he said. "More than you know."

He leaned in and stole a kiss. The unexpected action sent the pit of her stomach into a wild swirl. Before she had time to think about what it might mean, he was gone, headed toward the fellowship hall entrance and the fans who awaited him.

His newest fan sat in her car, a silly grin on her face.

# *Chapter Eleven*

Patrice had done her best cajoling with Reverend Baines and it wasn't working.

"I know you're Kara's sister, Patrice, but you aren't a member of Community Christian."

"But I'm a frequent visitor. I'm probably here more than some of the people on your church rolls."

He laughed. "That could very well be true. But you're not an official member. The choir singing with Mr. Ambrose is made up of church members. You wouldn't believe how many calls I've gotten from people who want to be a part of the mass choir. I can't set the precedent."

Patrice pouted, but accepted the minister's decision. "Can I at least stay and listen?"

Under the force of that smile, the minister relented.

Nodding, Cliff directed her to one of the pews in front. Because all of Community Christian's music groups were involved, the rehearsal had been moved to the sanctuary rather than the choir room.

Reverend Baines opened the rehearsal with prayer,

then turned the reins over to Matt, the church's music director.

"We're really blessed to have an artist of Marcus's stature working with us," he said.

"What about you?" someone said. "You were a national recording artist."

"Emphasis on the past tense," Matt said with a smile. He made a few announcements, explained their mission, then introduced Marcus.

Kara slipped in more than midway through the rehearsal. She recognized the song Marcus was teaching them as one from the tape that he'd lent her. Patrice stood right in front of him with the altos, though her range extended far beyond that one part.

Nancy Baines settled next to Kara on the back pew.

"And why aren't you up there?" the pastor's wife said. "You have a terrific voice."

"Patrice is the singer in the family. She has more natural talent than I'll ever possess. I see she talked Cliff into letting her in."

A glint of humor crossed Nancy's face. "Actually he didn't. He told her it was only open to members."

Kara looked alarmed. "Then what's she doing up there? I thought the rules…"

"They were doing a hymn, and I guess she was singing right along from her seat as they practiced. She must have lost herself in the music, because Marcus shushed everybody and Patrice was still sitting there, singing her heart out. You should have seen the look on his face as he watched her." Nancy smiled. "That's when the rules got bent."

Kara kept a pleasant smile on her face, though her insides twisted. She didn't have to see it to know the look Nancy described. Patrice had a way with men like that. And when her voice was added to the mix, especially with someone who'd made a career out of music, well, there was no competing.

Not, she told herself, that she was competing with her sister for Marcus. Nothing could be further from the truth.

"Kara, what's wrong?"

Some of her internal distress must have shown through the carefully constructed veneer she thought she'd put in place.

"May I ask you a question?"

Nancy patted her hand. "Of course. Anything."

"There's a poem with the question 'What happens to a dream deferred?'" Nancy nodded, encouraging her to go on. "Have you ever wondered what really happens to the dreams we defer?"

"I'm not following you, Kara."

Shaking her head, Kara reached for her purse. "I'm sorry. I was really thinking out loud."

On the drive to her mother's house she thought about her own lost dreams. Long ago she'd gotten over the resentment she had directed toward her parents, who hadn't allowed her to follow her own foolish dreams of a career in music. Instead of rebelling, she'd played by the good-daughter rules. And now, at thirty-one, she found herself wondering what could have been…if only.

Other things in her life took precedence now. She didn't usually allow herself the luxury of singing the "if only" blues. What she'd told Nancy was, however, true. Patrice had natural ability. Kara's was learned. Natural talent combined with practice and hard work would always outshine the other.

She let herself in the house and was surprised to find it empty. Kara made a cup of tea and carried the smiley-face mug into the family room. Marcus had asked her why she didn't sing. She did, though. All the time. She never got tired of lifting her voice in song, particularly praise songs. She'd just let go of the dream she'd once had of singing those songs in public, of having other people sing her music.

Putting the mug on a coaster, she sat at the piano and played a few of her favorite hymns. She switched to some of the classical compositions she'd played throughout high school, following endless piano lessons. Bach. Chopin. Beethoven. Then, effortlessly, she drifted into some of the music she'd written, melodies that only she and God cared about. She lifted her voice in song, giving thanks for life and abundant blessings as her hands flowed over the keys.

When she finished she sat there, spent but joyous.

"That was beautiful."

Kara yelped and whirled around, a scream on her mouth. A moment later the panic receded, even if her heart still beat like mad.

"Wh-what are you doing here?"

Marcus sat on the edge of the large overstuffed ottoman. "Enjoying a private concert."

Kara looked toward the door. She was known to get lost in herself when she played the piano, but not so much that she'd miss hearing the ruckus of the Spencer family's return. "Where's Patrice?"

"She went upstairs. We heard you playing when we came to the door." He got up, walked to the piano and leaned over the top. "She said if I didn't make a peep, I'd be in for a treat."

Kara looked in the direction of the upstairs.

"She said you don't like an audience. But after hearing you, I'm reminded that the Good Book says something about not hiding your lamp under a bushel."

"Not everyone is a performer, Marcus."

He stroked his goatee. "That's true. But you have a talent—"

"That's being put to use where it's needed most," Kara said. She closed the lid of the piano, effectively shutting off both the memories of her own deferred dreams and the conversation.

Marcus didn't try to convince her otherwise.

"I'm all changed," Patrice said, bopping into the room. She wore jeans, a cropped T-shirt and a pair of sand-colored mules that Kara had been searching for for weeks. "And I'm starving, too."

"Those look familiar," Kara said, indicating the shoes.

Patrice grinned. "I knew they'd look great on me. I'll return them. Promise," she said, crossing her heart with her fingers.

"Did the doctor okay you in heels yet?"

Patrice waved a hand, dismissing her sister's concern. "Can't look cute in flats, now, can I?"

"We're headed out for a bite," Marcus said. "Will you join us?"

Kara looked from her sister to Marcus. Three's a crowd. "No, that's all right. You guys go on."

"Come on, K. It'll be fun."

Kara doubted it, but she followed them.

Patrice picked the place, a loud game room/restaurant at the mall. Both Marcus and Kara looked dubious, but Patrice assured them it would be fun.

And it was, which is why the attack from Cyril that was in her morning newspaper came as a nasty shock.

### The Way I See It
### by Cyril Abercrombie
*Wayside Gazette* Community Columnist

That much-ballyhooed launch of a so-called community-service challenge between R & B superstar Marcus Ambrose and our own resident Dr. Do-Good was, it seems, just for show. Once the city television crews and the paparazzi jetted out of town, the pretense dropped like one of those fruitcakes the Wayside Revelers pawn off on us every holiday season.

Shame on you, Dr. Kara. We thought the *S* in your middle name stood for Substance, Style, Sincerity, or at the very least Sensible. Seems we've been proved wrong. Starstruck is more like it. Our month-long guest, who has spent more time holed up in a house he rented—right next door to Dr. K., we might add—than doing any of the promised work for the community, was seen on the town with not one, but two of Wayside's most eligible bachelorettes giggling on his arm.

Why is this notable, you might ask? Rare is it when the hit maker leaves behind his entourage—the size of which rivals the mayor's—or that fleet of black SUVs that make the quiet streets of Wayside appear to be overrun with organized crime bosses.

More followed, mostly in the way of biting jabs at the organizers of the film and music festival.

By the time she finished reading, Kara had moved beyond mild irritation and anger to pure rage. She slammed the newspaper down. "How dare he print that trash."

Her breakfast of hard-scrambled eggs and toast forgotten, Kara snatched up the newspaper and stormed out her back door. She met Marcus on the path halfway to her house, a copy of the *Gazette* balled up in his hand.

"I see you've read the morning paper."

"I can't believe Cyril would do such a dirty thing. And my middle name *doesn't* start with *S*. It's Lynette."

"In my experience, the best thing to do is just let these things blow over."

Kara issued an unladylike snort in response to that. "You don't live here," she said. "After you're packed up and gone, I still have to face all the people who read this garbage."

She whirled around and headed toward her car.

"Kara, where are you going?"

"To give that so-called journalist a piece of my mind."

"In your robe and slippers?"

Kara looked down and wanted the earth to open and swallow her whole.

She didn't know what could be more embarrassing—being caught in pj's or being caught in the pj's she was wearing.

It took twenty minutes to get dressed, but much longer to get over the fact that she'd stomped out of the house on such a tear that Marcus had seen her in a purple chenille robe that had, of course, seen better days, and rainbow bunny slippers—a birthday gift from Garrett.

It could have been worse, she figured. She could have been wearing some of the silky, slinky stuff she usually donned for lounging.

"Don't say one word," she said as she got into her car. Marcus, fully dressed in slacks and a loose shirt, grinned.

"But I really liked the slippers."

Fully and appropriately clothed now in slacks, a mauve twinset and conservative pumps, she started her car and drove straight to the newspaper office. She entered the reception area of the *Wayside Gazette* with Marcus.

He'd grinned when she'd come out her door, and had, from the twitch still evident at his mouth, been dying to say something else.

"I don't want to hear it, Marcus. I was upset."

"I'm just standing here," he'd said. But the smile in his voice had belied his innocence.

"I'd like to see Cyril Abercrombie, please," Kara said at the reception desk.

The young receptionist's mouth dropped open at the sight of Marcus. She paid no attention to Kara.

"You're him."

Marcus lounged into his playboy role, resting a hip against the counter. Kara nudged him. "We came to see Cyril."

"I can't believe you're standing here! Right at my desk. Wait till I tell everybody. I have all your CDs. Love them." She burst into the chorus of "Something about Your Smile," one of his latest hits.

Kara rolled her eyes.

The receptionist snatched up a piece of paper from her cluttered desktop. "May I have your autograph?"

"Sure thing. We've come to see Cyril Abercrombie."

"Take a number," she said. "The phones have been ringing off the hook all morning."

"Is he here?" Kara asked.

The young woman looked at Kara with a "when did you get here" expression. "Oh. Oh, dear." She picked up a phone. "Mrs. Everett, there are some people here to see you. Dr. Kara and Marcus Ambrose."

"My last name is Spencer," Kara interjected.

"What's your name, sweetheart?" Marcus said, plucking a pen from the jammed holder on her desk.

"Vickie. With an *i-e*. I'm your number one fan."

"Are you?" he said with that disarming smile Kara had come to recognize as his public persona. "Well, that's great to hear. Thanks for listening to my music."

He wrote something out to her and handed the paper and pen back.

Vickie clutched it to her heart. "Oh, my goodness. I can't believe it."

Kara muttered something that had Marcus glancing to his side.

The editor of the paper came out of her office to greet them. "Kara, I'm sorry about what got in the paper today." She introduced herself to Marcus, shook hands and led them into her office.

"So when did the *Gazette* become a supermarket tabloid?"

The editor winced. "You don't know just how on the mark you are. Cyril resigned this morning. Called me at home at 6:00 a.m to tell me he'd gotten another job. At a tabloid in Florida."

"Great," Kara said. "So I get to be his parting shot."

"I can't tell you how much I regret that that column got in the paper unedited," Mrs. Everett said. "I don't know how we missed it. I've already talked to his editor, as well as the features editor, who is going to do some damage control himself. You're not the only disgruntled readers. We're a small community paper and we can't afford to unnecessarily antagonize people."

"So what are you going to do?"

"Well, we've decided to do some new feature stories that we didn't already have planned. Is that all right?" She asked the question of Marcus.

"I'm not the one who needs to be appeased," he said. "I'm used to those kinds of fiery darts."

Kara looked at him, taken aback for a moment by his choice of words, straight from Ephesians. He did that a lot—quoted from the Bible without sounding as if he did.

"They come with the territory," he said. "And I've seen a lot worse. Dr. Spencer, on the other hand, is the one who was attacked unjustly. She shouldn't have to suffer for my notoriety."

Kara stared at him, surprised by both his defense of her and the quiet strength of his words. And she'd noticed the respect in his voice when he'd referred to her as Dr. Spencer, not the teasing "Dr. Kara."

The newspaper editor nodded. "I thought you'd

feel that way. I've already drafted an editor's note for the next edition.''

She handed Kara a piece of paper. Not quite an apology and not quite a correction, it acknowledged that Cyril Abercrombie's ''The Way I See It'' column had veered sharply away from its usual content and tone, and that both the column and the writer wouldn't be appearing in the newspaper's pages again.

''People will come to the conclusion you fired him.''

''People come to conclusions no matter what we do.''

''She's right, Kara.''

She looked at Marcus as if divining the truth. When he nodded, Kara sighed and handed the page to the editor. ''What about the factual error?'' Kara explained about her name, and Mrs. Everett promised to add that to the editor's note.

When Marcus led Kara from the office, she remained unsettled.

''How about some breakfast?'' Marcus asked back at her car.

Kara, still feeling vaguely dissatisfied by the entire encounter, slipped behind the wheel. ''I don't understand why he'd do that. We've had a good working relationship in the years he's been here.''

''I've found that it's not a productive exercise to try to determine what motivates people. You reap what you sow.''

She faced him. ''You never fail to surprise me, Marcus.''

He tugged on his seat belt. ''Why is that?''

''You're like two different people. Again.''

"I don't suffer from schizophrenia, if that's what you're angling toward. Everybody has different faces, Kara. A public one and a private one. The man I am when I perform is different from the one who takes his boots off at the end of the day."

"But isn't that—" she waved a hand searching for the right word "—disjointed?"

"Maybe. But it's a coping mechanism. The night we met, you painted a broad brush on people in the entertainment industry. In this case, I think that public/private persona issue applies to a lot—maybe not all, but a lot—of creative people. Look at Barbra Streisand. She has that wonderful voice and stage fright. There are countless actors who have speech impediments and stuttering problems, but when you turn on the cameras or light up the stage those impediments fade away as they assume the roles of the characters they portray. And look at writers, many of whom are sometimes introverts, but can become the life of a party."

"I never thought about it that way," she said as she pulled out of the parking lot.

He ran a gentle finger down the side of her face and tugged on a curl. "It'll be okay, Kara. You'll see."

And she believed him.

"Is that how you're received everywhere you go? With people falling all over themselves to tell you how much they love you?"

He gave her a pointed look. "Not everywhere. That's one of the reasons I like you."

She licked her lips and glanced at him. "I never know when you're being serious and when you're making fun."

"I'd never make fun of you."

Something in his eyes confirmed that. "Thank you," she said, the words barely a whisper.

He reached for her hand. "He had a point, you know."

"Who?"

"The former *Wayside Gazette* columnist."

Her hackles rose. "And that would be?"

"The challenge we issued."

"*You* issued a challenge. I got caught up in the media back draft. Besides, you did your time at the build-a-home site in East Wayside."

"Your friend Mr. Abercrombie must have been out of town that day."

She took her eye off the road to look at him.

"Do you care?"

The abrupt change of subject startled him. "About what?"

"What people say about you. It has to be pretty awful always having what you do broadcast to the world."

"Is this another therapy session?"

Kara's face fell. "I thought we were just having a conversation, getting to know each other better."

She reached for the gearshift, and his hand closed over hers. "It's not what people say that matters, Kara. It's just very hard to learn to trust."

"You trust all of those people you have on your staff."

"I've vetted every one of them. It's not staff that I worry about."

She looked into his eyes briefly and her breath caught. Something there sent her heart racing. Despite her best attempts to distance herself from Marcus, Kara found herself drawn to him in ways that transcended all of her other semirelationships. The admission might come from a place deep inside, but she was beginning to realize she was more than half in love with this man.

She'd always thought that she would fall headlong in love, the emotion bursting through her like a star going supernova. This thing with Marcus, though, snuck up on her when she wasn't looking, an awareness flowing through her strong and sure like a steadily moving river.

"Kara, are you all right?"

She blinked, remembered to breathe and looked at him. "I'm fine. Just fine." But her hands trembled on the steering wheel. She glanced at him again, knowing he must wonder about her odd behavior. "Where would you like to go for breakfast?"

"How about 24 Brandywine?"

"That's where you live."

"I can't do much in a kitchen, but I make a mean omelette."

The next day Erica celebrated her eighteenth birthday. Kara finished wrapping the earrings she'd gotten her as a little something extra. The family had all gone in to surprise her with a car. Garrett, still complaining about the unfairness of it all, met Kara at the door.

"Why does she get a car?"

Kara rubbed her baby brother's head. "Because she's eighteen and you're just fourteen. Because she has a job, and you don't. Because she's headed to college in Seattle soon, and you're not."

Garrett huffed.

Marcus was in the kitchen with Ida. They stopped talking the minute Kara walked in.

"What are you two up to?"

Ida wiped her hands on a towel. "Nothing, baby. Don't you look like an angel today."

"Mom." She'd spent an hour dressing—for Marcus to notice, not her mother.

White eyelet lace flecked with gold trimmed the bodice, short sleeves and hem of the chemise dress. She'd taken special care with her hair, and her skin radiated with a glow that came from a silky lotion with golden shimmers in it. Erica may have been the birthday girl, but Kara looked the part.

"I agree," he said. "And love the shoes."

Kara flushed straight to her toes visible through see-through gold sandals. She definitely had a thing for shoes, and since he kept noticing, he must have a fetish. Her jammed closet had so many shoes that Patrice used it as a supply center. Liberally. Today's pair of high heels had come straight from Milan, via the upscale shoe store she frequented in Portland.

"Thanks. Why am I not surprised to see you here?"

"Marcus is always welcome," Ida said. "Why don't you two help me take these to the table."

After Erica's birthday dinner with family and following a few stern reminders from Ida, Erica left for a night out with her friends in her new car. "I have an announcement to make," Patrice said, popping up.

All eyes turned toward her. She radiated excitement, and couldn't keep her eyes off Marcus.

"I've been dying to say something. Can I now?"

He shrugged.

Patrice dashed around the table and threw her arms around his shoulders and planted a huge kiss on him.

''I love this man!''

Kara's dessert fork clattered to her plate.

# Chapter Twelve

Ida, looking alarmed, was first to get words out. "What do you mean you love him?"

Patrice hugged Marcus. "He's everything and he's made me so happy."

Marcus squirmed in his seat. "Patrice..."

"Excuse me, please," Kara said, pushing her chair back so suddenly that it threatened to topple over. With an unsteady hand she righted it and hastened from the room.

Gordon motioned to Ida, who followed Kara.

"Kara, honey?"

She ran upstairs, realizing too late she no longer lived here or had a refuge or bedroom to run to.

The bathroom. She shut and locked the door and leaned on it, her breath coming in short gasps, her heart racing as if she'd run a marathon.

Ida's knock came a moment later.

"Kara, honey, please open the door."

"I need a minute, Mom."

She'd need more than a minute to get herself together. The pain hurt like a band constricting her heart, like splinters under nails. At that moment she realized she'd done more than fallen halfway in love with Marcus Ambrose. She'd fallen all the way, hard, deep and fast. And to what avail?

He was in love with Patrice.

Intellectually, Kara knew that her sister could make Marcus happy. She was pretty and vibrant and sang as if heaven was on fire. Patrice wouldn't be relegated to the role of backstage spouse. She'd be right in front, singing with him.

"Kara, I'm sure there's a good explanation. Let me in, please."

Swallowing hard, she opened the door. Ida took one look at her and wrapped her in her arms.

"Oh, baby. You love him, don't you?"

Sniffling and nodding, Kara mumbled, "Uh-huh."

"You know how Patrice is. Next week she'll have forgotten all about him, on to her next crush."

"She's loved him forever. She used to spend hours gazing at his posters and dancing around like she was in his arms."

Ida tsked. "Patrice has never been truly in love. I'll know it when she is. You, on the other hand…" she said, lifting her daughter's chin. "You never let yourself go enough to fall in love before, so it's hit you doubly hard. I think Marcus has cut through all those defenses you've built up through the years."

"He doesn't care about me."

"That's not true," Ida said. "I've lived long enough to know when I see a man pursuing a woman. And I've talked to him. He's on the move, and has been since you knocked him off his feet at that debate. He has a good heart and he loves the Lord. That's what's important.''

''Loves the Lord? Marcus? He's Mr. Bump and Grind.''

Ida chuckled. ''That's all you've let yourself hear.'' She pulled a fluffy beige washcloth from a basket and wet the edge, then wiped Kara's face. ''You and Patrice used to go at it like cats and dogs about her music. And you remember what that music was, don't you?''

Kara nodded. ''Marcus Ambrose.''

''I think all you really disliked about it was the volume that Patrice played it. Did you ever listen to the words?''

Kara put the lid down and sat on the commode. Ida took a seat on the edge of the bathtub.

''I've heard the songs on the radio.''

''Umm-hmm. I bet you didn't know that every one of his records has a Christian tune on it.''

''Mom, please. There's nothing holy about 'Baby, I'm gonna make you sweat and moan.''' But she'd also heard his other music, music that had yet to be released.

Ida laughed. ''No, I suppose not on that one. That's just one of his hits. I did a little reading up, too, on your Mr. Ambrose.''

''He's not mine. He's Patrice's.''

Ida waved that off. ''I've a pretty good idea what that's all about. And it has nothing to do with here,'' she said, tapping her heart. ''There're some interesting things on the liner notes of his CDs.''

''Since when do you read liner notes?''

Leaning forward, Ida took Kara's hands. ''Since I realized your father and I made a mistake with you.

Watching Patrice through the years, and in talking to Marcus these last couple of weeks, I can see that clearly now. You were our first, Kara. Our beautiful baby girl. We didn't want to mess up with you.''

Ida smoothed the hair at Kara's temple. ''Keeping you on the straight and narrow, keeping you focused on the Lord's service was all your Dad and I knew to do. When we moved out here from South Carolina, we didn't know anybody. All we had to cling to was each other and the Lord. We didn't let you follow your own heart because we were too busy trying to make sure it never got broken.''

''What are you saying, Mom?''

Ida took a deep breath. ''We should have let you major in music like you wanted to.''

Kara shook her head. ''That was a long time ago. I've…''

Ida smiled, a little sadly. ''You've always been the diplomat, sugar. The one to soothe feathers and not rock the boat. We said, 'No.' You said, 'Okay.'''

Kara looked at her hands and mumbled, ''Like I had a choice.''

''That's just it,'' Ida said, lifting her chin. ''You always had a choice. You could obey or disobey. Looking back now, I know we were too hard on you. Your father and I learned with you and tried to do better by Ben and Faye, and then Patrice and Erica.''

''And Garrett gets away with murder.''

In spite of herself, Ida chuckled. ''The baby of the family always gets liberties. By the time he came along, we were tired and old.''

''You're not old.''

''And you're not going to give up on Marcus. He's a good man. He'll make you happy.''

Kara shook her head again. "You mean he'll make Patrice happy."

Ida shook her head. "I sure raised a stubborn child. Honey child, can't you see? He's just as hung up on you as you are on him. And he knows how to express it about as well as you do."

"I'm not hung up," she said, accenting the description with air quotes, "on Marcus Ambrose. And he's not on me. Trust me."

"Umm-hmm. That's why you're up here in the bathroom crying your eyes out."

She had a point there. "Well, that's just…"

Chuckling, Ida got up and pulled open a drawer on the vanity. She handed Kara a compact. "I got this the other day. Bought several of them because I thought they were so cute."

Kara opened the compact to reveal a makeup trio of foundation and blush. "What's this third one?"

"Concealer," Ida said. "It'll hide those tracks you were crying about that man downstairs—the one you don't care anything about."

Kara looked at the mini makeup kit and then at her mother. "Did I ever tell you how much I love you?"

"Yep. But I always like hearing it again."

By the time Kara got her face back together and returned downstairs, Marcus was gone. So, she noticed, was Patrice.

Someone had cleared the table of everything except the big German chocolate cake Ida had baked for Erica's birthday. Kara found Garrett in the den rifling through a collection of video games.

"Where'd everybody go?"

Garrett shrugged and powered up his game on the television. "Marcus said he had to do some errands, and Patrice went with him. Dad's outside looking at that tree branch that's hanging over the garage."

Still feeling out of sorts, Kara plopped onto the sectional and hugged a small quilted pillow to her breast.

"Wanna play?"

"Nah. Not right now."

"Guess what?" Garrett added. "Marcus is gonna put Patrice on his new CD."

Kara sat up. CD? Is that what the announcement was all about?

Patrice, given to hyperbole, *could* have been expressing her enthusiastic joy about that—not undying love for Marcus.

*Undying love?* Is that what she felt for him?

Hardly.

But what else could explain her meltdown?

As her brother obliterated hostile aliens from the planet, Kara thought about what her mother had said, and about her immediate and visceral reaction to Patrice's bold dinner announcement.

If what Garrett had said was true, and she had no reason to doubt it, Patrice would soon get to live her dream—the very one Kara had once harbored. Taking a deep breath, she told herself that she'd ultimately made the right decisions in her life.

She had a career she could be proud of. She'd traveled a bit. She wore great shoes.

Kara laughed in spite of herself.

"What?" Garrett said.

"Just thinking out loud, baby brother. Just thinking out loud."

In short, she'd been blessed to have come as far as she had. Many of her classmates hadn't been as fortunate. That strict upbringing by Ida and Gordon *had* kept her on the straight and narrow. And now, through the community grants she wrote, her volunteer work with the women's shelter and through the counseling she did, she was in a position to help people who weren't as fortunate.

That was something to be proud of.

Yet there lingered within Kara a tiny spark of "what if?" What if she'd taken the route toward a career in music? What if she'd been the one Marcus...

Kara thrust the pillow and the thoughts aside.

"I'll see you later, Garrett."

Twisting his body this way and that as he stalked aliens, Garrett just grunted.

Outside, Kara spied her father up on a ladder propped against the garage. Wielding a long-handled branch trimmer, he attacked the boughs with the same gusto with which Garrett slew his video invaders.

"Bye, Daddy."

He leaned over and smiled down at her. "You take care now, Kara. That Marcus is something else, isn't he?"

Kara heaved a sigh. "Yeah. Something else."

By the time Kara got home, another thought had coalesced regarding Marcus. What if he'd been using all of them? If he did keep himself surrounded by people in an effort to avoid loneliness, he'd managed to ingratiate himself with her family with no regard for the feelings and expectations he set up, whether intentionally or not.

The usual caravan of SUVs sat outside, with more cars and trucks parked along the curb and on the street. One blocked her driveway. In a surly mood, she pulled right in front of it, effectively trapping the driver in, and stomped to her house.

Two messages awaited, both from Howard.

Howard.

She hadn't given him or his proposal more than five minutes of thought since the day they'd had lunch. Feeling bad about that and knowing what she had to do, Kara returned the call, aiming to make it up to him.

"Will you accept a double order of shrimp Panang curry and coconut ice cream as an apology?" she asked him.

"Only if you toss in some lemongrass soup for an appetizer."

Kara smiled. Next to electronic gadgetry, Howard had one weakness—Thai food. "It's a deal," she said.

"I'll pick you up in ten minutes."

She was locking her front door when Patrice appeared out of nowhere.

"Hi, K."

"What are you doing here? I didn't see your car."

"I got a ride with one of the guys," Patrice said, indicating the house next door. "Marcus is throwing a party."

"I see."

"Aren't you coming?"

Kara adjusted the thin strap of her shoulder bag. "I have a date with Howard."

Patrice wrinkled her mouth. "I've never been quite sure what you see in him."

Before Kara had time to analyze that very thing for herself, Patrice had moved to another subject. ''What about Marcus?''

Headlights turned and then cast their glow across the two women, who turned to see who approached. Howard's sensible sedan came into view. Unable to get close because of all the parked vehicles, he double-parked and tooted the horn. ''Just a sec,'' Kara called to him. Then, to her sister she said, ''Marcus? You seem to have the Marcus front nailed down just fine. I'm very happy for you.'' She couldn't quite make that cheery.

''Kara, what's wrong?''

''Not a thing,'' she said. ''I know you'll make him happy.''

''Make him happy?''

But Kara was already at Howard's car. She slipped inside, waved to Patrice and tried not to look at 24 Brandywine, where all the lights were ablaze.

Long after the car had disappeared from view, Patrice stared after them, a contemplative expression on her pretty face.

''I think my analyst big sis has come to an incorrect diagnosis,'' she mused.


''I know what you're going to say,'' Howard said after they'd placed their orders.

''About what?''

''Us. It's not every day a guy issues a proposal.''

Kara reached for his hand. ''I know. And I'm sorry. I just—''

''I'm pretty boring. I know that. And I have a one-track mind.''

''That's not true,'' Kara said, feeling like a heel.

Then she smiled. "Well, the part about the one-track mind is true. But not the rest."

He patted his shirtfront and held out his hands. "Did you notice?"

Uh-oh. Kara really hated guessing games. "Notice what?"

"No PDA, no programming manual." He reached into his pants pocket. "Nothing except this." He pulled out a small gray velvet box and placed it on the table between them.

Kara's stomach did a painful flip. She covered her mouth with her hand. "I... Howard, this is..."

"Open it," he said.

She didn't touch the jeweler's box. She knew what she'd find inside and didn't know how to let this good man down. Once upon a time—like a month ago—Howard was everything she thought she wanted in a mate: hardworking, dedicated to church and home, professional, financially secure. That list now seemed so static, so antithetical to joy and light and... She realized she'd left love out of the original inventory.

Now she knew.

"Howard, I can't. I know this seemed like the inevitable conclusion to our relationship, but I'm not in love with you." The last came out sounding as miserable as Kara felt.

His smile was tender. "I know that, Kara."

She lifted her head, and her gaze met his. "Huh?"

He chuckled. "You know, in all the time we've been friends, I've never heard you say anything as inarticulate as 'huh?'"

Kara searched his face looking for a clue, some hint of just what was happening. Howard picked up the jeweler's box and offered it to her in his open palm.

"Open it, Dr. Kara."

She winced at the name, but opened the box. Inside, instead of the diamond solitaire she'd expected to see, twinkled two tiny computer chips.

"What is this?"

"Earrings," he said. "I had them made for you. Each one is a real chip, but there's a gold overlay." He shrugged. "I just wanted you to remember me."

"Oh, Howard." She closed her hand around his. "I'm sorry."

"Don't be sorry, Kara. I knew when I floated that halfhearted proposal over at the inn that this, us, wasn't really an 'us.' You didn't turn cartwheels in the aisles and I wasn't being very romantic about what's supposed to be a lifetime commitment."

"So what now?"

The server appeared with spring rolls and sauce and placed them on the table.

"Now we eat."

She stayed his hand when he reached for a small plate to serve her. "I'm serious, Howard."

He clasped her hands in his. "Now we remain friends. And you wear those earrings every now and then. Deal?"

Kara took out the small gold hoops in her ears and replaced them with the computer chips. "Deal."

At Marcus's house Patrice had him trapped in the pantry.

"We need to talk about Kara."

"What about her?" Marcus said, inching his way around Patrice.

"She thinks we're an us."

Marcus shook his head. "There is no us, Patrice."

"I know that. You know that. But Kara doesn't."

"Your sister might be a therapist, but she's the one who needs to be on an analyst's couch."

Patrice grinned. "She loves you, too."

Marcus stopped. "I need to get back to my guests." Then he walked away from her.

Patrice threw up her hands and appealed to the ceiling. "Lord, you gotta help me here with these two clueless folks."

The party, in full swing, had a mix of Wayside townspeople, Marcus's neighbors on the street whom Nadira had been careful to invite so they wouldn't complain about noise, Marcus's staff and band members and some of the choir members from Community Christian.

He'd managed an escape from Patrice, only to have Nadira corral him just when he'd made it to the piano.

"Marcus, I think you need to talk to Teddy. He's holed up in his bedroom and won't come out."

"What's wrong with him?"

Nadira shrugged. "You know how he gets."

Marcus did know. Teddy, his backup driver and Nadira's gofer, like Marcus suffered from bouts of self-doubt. Marcus's were a result of worrying that he'd never fulfill his mission in life. Teddy, another victim of childhood abandonment, had other issues.

"Has he been taking his medication?"

"Marcus, my hands are full making sure you get everywhere you're supposed to be. I can't baby-sit twenty-five other people, as well."

He placed a hand on her shoulder. "I'm sorry. I should have realized. How's your father doing?"

Nadira spent her off time back in Los Angeles, where her father was dying of pancreatic cancer. If he hadn't been preoccupied with thoughts of the aggravating Dr. Kara Spencer he'd have noticed the circles under his assistant's eyes and the telltale signs of tension. Nadira, a woman of infinite patience and organization, fiercely guarded his privacy and his time. And she never snapped at him—even when he deserved it.

"Not well," she said. "The doctors said three more months at the most."

He noticed the smallest change in Kara Spencer's mood, the way her eyes sparkled with humor or irritation. Yet he'd missed the lines at this woman's eyes. Nadira had been by his side for years, keeping his world organized and his business affairs aligned. She looked as if she would collapse any moment, and he'd never even noticed. Marcus pulled her to him for a hug.

"Go home, Nadira. That's where you belong."

She shook her head. "Who's going to stay with you?"

"Don't worry about that. You get on a flight in the morning and stay with your dad as long as you need to."

She hugged him back. "Thanks, Marcus. I don't know how much help Teddy will be to you, so I'll pull Sheldon and Leonard from the hotel and send them here." Pulling a slim PDA from a hidden pocket, she jotted down a few notes. "I've already extended the meals contract with Amber Montgomery, so there's food in the house."

Marcus plucked the stylus from her hand. "Radar, I can take care of myself. You go take care of you."

She nodded. He handed her the stylus. "Thank you, Marcus. I'll go book a flight."

Someone tugged on his sleeve. Marcus turned. Recognizing one of his Brandywine Street neighbors, he turned on the charm.

Marcus the entertainer played the piano for his guests, and promised everyone house seats at the benefit concert if they brought five paying people who donated to the scholarship fund-raiser. Then he introduced Patrice as his newest protégé.

Much later, after all the guests had left for their houses or hotel rooms, Marcus sat on his back porch steps nursing a bottle of strawberry-flavored spring water.

"I didn't appreciate your guests blocking my driveway."

He looked up.

Kara stood there, a plastic bag dangling from her hand.

He somehow felt drained, weary of doing battle with her. So he ignored the taunt. "Patrice found your spare key and moved your car."

"So you're going to take her under your wing?"

He nodded. "Something like that."

"Don't you break her heart, Marcus. I know you don't care about me at all, but you better not mess with my sister."

A phone rang somewhere in Marcus's house, the ring loud in the still night.

"I'll be out of your town and your life in a week. I think we can manage to not get in each other's way during that time."

Kara didn't say anything, then she turned to go.

"Marcus?"

"What?"

A scream rent the air before she could say anything else.

Marcus leaped up, Kara dropped her bag and they both sprinted into his house.

A woman's screams carried through the house. They took the stairs at a run and found Teddy in Nadira's room. She clutched the phone in one hand, and tears streamed down her face.

"What happened?"

"I don't know," Teddy said. "I was going to the bathroom and I heard her hollering."

Marcus went to Nadira, pulled the phone from her hand and gathered her in his arms. Kara, not sure what to do, took the phone receiver.

"Hello? This is Dr. Kara Spencer. I'm with Nadira and Marcus. Could you please tell me what's happened?"

Kara listened on the line for a moment, then confirmed what Marcus had already guessed. "Her father," she said softly. "He died an hour ago at Wellspring Hospice in Los Angeles."

Though she'd spoken quietly and carefully and for Marcus's benefit, Nadira must have heard, because the woman's wails increased. Marcus sank to the floor, holding her.

"Yes, I'll tell her," she said to the person on the line at the hospice. Kara found the phone receiver and set to rights the telephone and book that had fallen to the carpet.

For all her skills, Kara was ill prepared to deal with grief. She'd been to a few funerals, but no one close to her had ever died. Both sets of grandparents were in their seventies, but vibrant and active. Kara didn't know how she'd cope if something happened to her own father.

"I'm sorry," she began.

Marcus shook his head. This wasn't the time for platitudes.

"They said to tell her about the insurance. It won't cover some things."

Another moan came from Nadira. Kara looked around, spied a box of tissue and brought it over, handing some to the woman, who balled them up in her hand. "The doctors said three months. He had another three months."

Fresh tears flowed and tears came to Kara's eyes—her own grief at the other woman's pain. Kara sat on the edge of the bed. She put a hand on Marcus's shoulder as he rocked and ministered to his assistant. They sat that way for what seemed like a long, long time.

"He's winging it up to heaven right now," Marcus said eventually. "And that's a good place to be. You know he's laughing and smiling and giving St. Peter grief at the tollgate. Probably bending his ear with that story about how he rescued a village in Kuwait and how that ought to pay his fee into heaven."

A strangled sound, a cross between a laugh and a sob, emerged from Nadira.

"And he's not in pain anymore. You were worried about that, weren't you?"

She nodded, sniffling.

"Hey, Nadira. I'm sorry," Teddy said. "I didn't

know your pops, but, you know… If you need something…''

She nodded, and Teddy made his escape from the room.

Marcus glanced at his wrist, then realized he wasn't wearing a watch. ''What time is it?'' he said over his shoulder.

''Just after two,'' Kara said.

He stroked Nadira's head. ''Are you all packed?'' She nodded.

''I knew I should have kept the plane up here on standby.''

''It's not cost-effective….''

Marcus hugged Nadira. ''Listen to you. Don't you worry about that. Or about whatever you need. I'll take care of everything.''

''I can't ask you to do that,'' Nadira said. ''My sister and I…''

''Will be there for each other and the bills come to me. End of story.''

She nodded and reached for a tissue.

''I could get John up here,'' Marcus said. ''But it's going to take him about three hours to get to the hangar and then get up here from L.A. We could drive, but that'll take even longer. What time was your flight?''

''Ten-thirty. Northwest via Alaska Air.''

Nadira shifted and moved to get up. Kara lent her a hand.

''Tell you what. I'll get that changed to the earliest one they have out of here and you try to get some rest. Okay?''

Still looking dazed, Nadira said, ''I need to call my sister.''

"All right. Kara, would you stay with her while I go call the airline?"

"Marcus?"

He turned back to Nadira.

"Thank you." She wrapped her arms around him and they stood together for a long time. Kara felt like an intruder, disrupting a private moment.

As if to illustrate just that, after Marcus went to make the call the two women stood together awkwardly.

*Lord, show me what to do.*

Kara's entreaty silently went up. In addition to not knowing Nadira, she held the guilt of initially harboring less than charitable thoughts toward the woman.

"I'm sorry for your loss," she told Nadira.

"It's just not fair." Nadira closed her eyes and rubbed them. "I was headed down there tomorrow to stay with him. They said three more months."

New tears fell. Not knowing what else to do, Kara took the other woman's hand and squeezed it.

"I need to call Najila."

"Would you like me to stay with you?"

Nadira nodded. The two women hugged, and then Nadira called her younger sister. Kara's heart broke again as she listened to Nadira's tearful explanation.

After the phone call Kara wet a washcloth and brought it to Nadira, who was curled up in bed clutching a pillow.

"Would you like a cup of tea or something?"

"Thank you for staying. I know you didn't have to do that."

"I wanted to," Kara said. And she knew the statement to be the truth.

Kara didn't know much about grief, but she did know about the power of prayer. Whether this woman would be receptive to it was something else. "Would you let me pray with you?"

# *Chapter Thirteen*

When Nadira nodded, Kara smiled. She went to the edge of the bed and got on her knees. Holding the other woman's hands, she prayed for her strength.

"Father God, we come to You with bowed heads and open hearts. There's a need here now. You know the pain and grief being felt by Nadira and her family at this moment. Lord, we know You have everything in control. We ask You to send a measure of comfort and peace here now. Nadira and Najila need Your strength and Your power to get them through this dark night. We know, Father, that weeping endures for just a night and You bring joy in the morning. Thank You, Lord, for Your grace and for Your mercy. All these blessings we ask in Your Son's name."

Together the two women said, "Amen."

Kara brushed Nadira's hair back from her brow. "I'll go get that tea for you."

Still dressed, Nadira shifted under the sheet.

"Dr. Kara?"

At the door Kara paused.

"Will you look after him while I'm away?"

Kara's face must have registered the question she didn't voice.

"Marcus," Nadira explained. "Will you?"

Kara didn't know what type of looking after a grown man needed, but she nodded her assent nonetheless.

Downstairs Marcus sat at the kitchen table, his hands wrapped around a mug of coffee. Kara glanced at the counter where a coffeemaker sat.

"I thought you didn't drink coffee."

"I don't," he said. "I just like the smell of it."

Guessing at the right cabinet, Kara found a mug, filled it with water from the tap and put it in the microwave.

"She and her sister have beautiful names."

Marcus nodded. "Their dad spent a lot of time in the Middle East working in the oil fields back in the seventies and eighties. Nadira's name means rare or precious, and I think she told me once that her sister's means brilliant or beautiful eyes."

Seeing that he, too, was affected by the night's events, Kara put her arm around his shoulders. "You're a good friend to her."

"Not as good as I should have been."

"What do you mean?"

"This is my fault. She should have been there with him." He glanced at her and shook his head. "Had I been a better friend, a better employer, I would have realized that she needed some time. I've been so focused on me that I haven't paid attention to the people around me, the people who depend on me."

"That's not true," Kara said. "I've seen you in

action. You care a lot about other people. I saw you
with Nadira tonight. And I saw you with those choir
members at church, and with fans on the street. You
give and give, Marcus. If you're selfish, it's with the
time you spend with yourself."

"How would you know about the time I spend on
me?"

The microwave pinged. Kara got up and dropped
in a tea bag found in a small box in the pantry. Placing the cup and saucer on a tray that bore Amber's
Appetizers & More logo, she turned to Marcus. "I
know because whether you realize it or not, you're
always looking out for other people. You've done
that from the very first night I met you."

When she returned to the kitchen, Marcus still sat
at the table. "She's asleep. I guess I'll head home."

She wanted to stay, but didn't know how to ask.
She wanted to comfort him, but didn't have the
words. His head was bent and he stared into his cup.
She placed a hand on his shoulder, then headed to
the back door.

"Dr. Kara?"

She'd pushed the screen door open, but now
paused.

"Thank you for being here."

Outside, Kara found the bag of leftover Pad Thai
right where she'd dropped it. She chucked the bag
into the trash bin, then made her way upstairs.

At his kitchen table, Marcus felt some of the old
insecurity creeping in on him. There'd been a time
when he'd been anything but the man with the confident image he publicly projected. Maybe Kara was

right. Maybe ultimately it wasn't healthy to wear so many different faces.

He thought about how she'd handled herself tonight—with quiet dignity through the long hours. The woman Kara had been upstairs with Nadira was the same woman no matter the circumstance. She didn't know Nadira, didn't have to stay. A part of him wondered why she had, though another part close to his heart already knew the reason.

He tried to pray, but his mind, cluttered with guilt about not being attentive to Nadira and with details of the day's events, refused to focus.

Earlier, Patrice had dropped a bombshell on him. Two, actually.

*She loves you, too.*

The *too* part is what got him.

Did Patrice see or sense in him something he hadn't even admitted to himself? He'd fallen in love with Kara Spencer, and her compassion tonight—shown toward someone she didn't even know—just further illustrated why he'd come to love her in so little time.

The thought of truly loving someone—and everything it might mean—frightened him. All of his professional life he'd surrounded himself with the accoutrements and the melodies of love, but he didn't have a real-life application by which to measure it.

Theory and application weren't mutually exclusive.

And furthermore, could Patrice have really meant that Kara loved him—was in love with him?

That hardly seemed likely.

But the image of her smiling up at him, laughing with him, kissing him, made him wonder.

Instead of being a singer, Patrice Spencer should have considered acting. A layer of drama compounded everything she said and did. Like the other night at dinner when Kara had taken ill. Patrice had hopped up at that table and announced that he'd agreed to let her sing on his next production.

He smiled. Patrice's enthusiasm would be a boon when the time came to do the hard work necessary to produce and then promote her own projects. It would take an exceptional man to keep up with her frenetic pace. She had the talent to become a star and the disposition of a diva. But did she have the work ethic and the determination to see it all to fruition?

That night at the Spencers' house, he'd wanted to check on Kara, to tell her how he felt, but the evening hadn't quite worked out the way he'd planned. After assurance from Gordon that Kara was fine and that Ida tended to her, Marcus had let himself be dragged out of the house by Patrice.

Twice now he'd hesitated when Kara had been receptive. He'd missed a chance then and had blown an opportunity tonight to tell Kara how he felt about her. To tell her she was the song in his heart and the melody of a praise psalm.

Her sister's views notwithstanding, where he was concerned, Kara seemed to run hot and cold.

He got up and stared out the back door. Dawn would break across the night horizon soon.

''Go to bed,'' he told himself. Maybe hearing the words would spur the action.

Losing himself to sleep had to be better than beating himself up for not being more receptive to Nadira's needs or sitting around feeling like a loser because he couldn't seem to win over one woman.

He shut and locked the back door and turned off the coffeemaker, but he couldn't shut out or turn off the thoughts of Kara.

He'd stood at the door while she prayed with Nadira. And he marveled at her ability to be both a comfort and a minister at the same time. But what did he really have to offer someone like Kara? Wealth and fame didn't count for much. Kara had been less than impressed with either one. And neither his money nor his celebrity could bring Nadira's father back.

For the first time, Marcus doubted the calling and direction of his life.

After the night's events, Kara thought her afternoon with Haley at the Olde Towne cemetery an appropriate outing.

"If we can finish cataloging this section, Eunice and Nora will do the last one."

The Wayside Historical Committee's five-year effort to get all of the interred identified with markers would soon wrap up. The committee worked alongside the genealogy group that met once a month at the library. Today Kara and Haley were armed with cameras, a grid and metal detectors on loan from a metal detector enthusiast who hadn't been able to join them. The equipment was used to locate metal buttons on clothing, coins that were sometimes buried with prospectors, or even rivets on long-buried caskets of the well-to-do deceased. Haley, her blond hair drawn back in a ponytail and tied with a mint-green scarf, pulled a wire basket on wheels, which toted their supplies.

She peered into the distance. "Is that Marcus Ambrose?"

Kara turned, shielding her eyes from the sun. "Where?"

Pointing, Haley directed her. "Over there." She consulted the grid they used. "In the Garden of Memories."

Kara put her gear into the basket, and the women headed toward the solitary figure in black who stood among the graves near a grove of cherry trees. It *was* Marcus. He stood at a gravestone, touched it and then moved to another.

"What's he doing?" Haley whispered.

His movement seemed almost reverent, his steps deliberate.

"Wait here. I'll go see." When Kara got close enough, she called quietly so as not to startle him. "Marcus?"

He looked up, and Kara's breath caught. He didn't try to hide the tears that streamed down his face.

Kara quickly closed the space between them. "What's wrong?"

He shook his head and looked away.

Looking for a clue, Kara read the closest headstone, the last one he'd touched, its lettering faded but readable.

Matilde Jeffries
1864-1891
A good woman

Kara glanced up at him. Was he crying over a woman who'd been dead more than one hundred years? Had she been a relative of his? Or was this a residual effect of the death of Nadira's father?

She reached for his hand. "Marcus?"

"I'd like some time alone, Kara."

Stung, she dropped her hand and backed up a step. "All right. I didn't mean to intrude."

"Kara, wait."

"You've made yourself pretty clear," she said.

Kara made her way back to the place where Haley stood waiting.

"What's wrong?"

She shrugged, not willing to say anything, feeling very much as if she'd desecrated hallowed ground. "He's just...he's... We should go."

He called, but got her machine. He opted against leaving a message. What, after all, would he say? *Kara, sorry you saw me crying like a little boy. Nadira's grief and my own loneliness got the better of me.*

Instead, he boarded the jet that would take him home to L.A.—to business that couldn't be put off any longer and to the assistant who needed a friend at her side. While his charter pilot set a course south, Marcus sat back, his eyes closed, his mind focused and his fingers on the minikeyboard he kept on the plane. Then he wrote an homage to a good woman. Not the long-gone Matilde Jeffries whose headstone had inspired the title, but to Kara Spencer, who inspired him to greater heights.

At 22 Brandywine Street, Kara paced the floor worrying about Marcus. She waited for him to come home or for one of his crew to show up. She wanted to inquire about Nadira, to maybe get an address where she could send a sympathy card. But mostly she was concerned about Marcus and wanted to make sure he was all right. If he somehow blamed himself for the death of Nadira's father, he'd be in a fragile state of mind.

But no one ever showed up at the house next door. Not a single one of the luxury SUVs put in a driveway appearance.

When her phone rang she snatched it up, hoping it was Marcus.

"Is Marcus there?" Kara raised an eyebrow at Patrice's question.

"No," she said, glancing out the window, willing his black SUV to pull into the adjacent drive. "Why would he be?"

"He canceled the rehearsal this afternoon at the church. I thought maybe you two were playing hooky together."

In that moment all of Kara's fears coalesced. Fear of what it meant to be in love with someone like Marcus. Anger at the way he'd brushed her off at the cemetery. Concern for Nadira. Stress about the way she was stressing. And irritation at Patrice's persistent cheerfulness.

"I'm not his keeper," she snapped.

"Well, there's no need to get an attitude about it. I was just asking a question. Teddy said you guys drank that nasty tea together sometimes, so I thought he might be at your house."

So now she was the topic of speculation among his staff. Kara lost what little patience she had left. The stress from the night before, the sting of Marcus's repeated rejection and the futile feelings she had for him all roiled inside her until she erupted in temper and irritation.

"Grow up, why don't you, Patrice? Your Miss Merry Sunshine routine gets on my nerves. I've told you before and I'm tired of repeating myself on this Marcus Ambrose thing. Stop pestering me about him."

"You're just jealous! My singing career is going somewhere and yours isn't."

"Well, at least I have brains to fall back on."

"You're mean and hurtful and I hate you." Patrice slammed the phone down in her ear. It took all of three seconds for Kara to feel awful. Quickly she dialed the number to her parents' house. The line was busy.

"Come on, Patrice. I'm sorry." She dialed again and still got a busy tone. She tried her sister's cell, which rang.

"Hello?" a sniffly voice said.

"Patrice. Please. I'm sor—"

The phone clicked off.

Kara sighed.

She called her mother's cell number.

"The wireless customer you are trying to reach is unavailable at this time. Please try your call again later."

Kara bowed her head. She shouldn't have taken her frustrations out on her sister. Patrice had an exuberant spirit, some of which Kara could have used at the moment. And with all her upcoming plans to sing with Marcus, maybe Patrice had her own set of stressors that put her on edge even more than usual.

This wasn't something she could let fester. Despite the children's ditty "Sticks and stones may break my bones, but words will never hurt me,'' Kara knew it wasn't true. Words could hurt. They could be among the worst of weapons, and once spoken could never be taken back. All she could do now was ask for forgiveness.

Grabbing her car keys, purse and cell phone, she headed to her mother's house. In a few minutes she was three blocks from her parents' place. She tried the cell again, and Ida answered.

''What in the world is going on? There's been a lot of yelling and door slamming going on around here. What happened?''

''I lost my temper.'' Kara pulled into the Spencer driveway. ''We both said some things we shouldn't have.''

''She said you called her stupid.''

''I didn't call her stupid, Mom.''

''Well, you two need to sort this out. I expect this sort of thing from Erica. But you, Kara? Really.''

Kara flipped the phone shut. ''Is Patrice still here?''

Ida yelped, whirled around and clutched her chest. Kara stood in the kitchen doorway, pocketing her cell phone. ''I wish you all would stop doing that.''

''Patrice?''

''She's up in her room.''

Kara took the stairs two at a time. She knocked on her sister's door. ''Patrice? It's me. Open up, please. I'm sorry.''

''Go away.''

''What's all the yelling about?'' Garrett asked.

''Your sisters had a fight,'' Gordon said.

''Really? Who won?'' Garrett turned and headed toward the door where Kara knocked, but Gordon caught him by the scruff of the neck and tugged him away.

"This is for the girls to settle. You need to go do your chores."

"I already washed the car."

"And the van?"

Garrett groaned. So did Kara, but for an entirely different reason. Patrice's muffled crying could be heard through the portal.

"Patrice, please. Let me in. I didn't mean those things."

"Yes, you did. You always think before you say things."

Not this time she hadn't. Yelling through the door wouldn't get her anywhere, so Kara retreated to consider another approach.

She found her mother sitting at the dining-room table flipping through the pages of an *Ebony* magazine. "I made a mess of things," Kara said.

Ida nodded. "People do that."

"I hurt her feelings."

"Yes, you did."

"I tried to apologize, but she wouldn't let me."

Ida closed the magazine, pushed it aside and looked at her daughter. "There's more going on here than an argument with your sister. You two used to go at it like champions when you were younger."

"I'm supposed to be an adult now."

Ida just looked at her. Realizing what she'd just said, Kara closed her eyes for a moment. "I've been treating Patrice like a child, the way I did when I was seventeen and she was a ten-year-old messing with my clothes and makeup. She's just as much of a grown-up as I am."

"Yes. Just because she lives at home isn't a reason to treat her like you would Erica or Garrett."

"Even Erica's getting up there. Soon you and Daddy will have the place all to yourselves."

Ida nodded. "I've got the renovation plans tucked under my bed. I get a spa and a sewing room and your father gets a study and a workshop. We'll leave one bedroom available. That'll discourage you all from showing up ten years from now with spouses and children in tow."

Kara stared slack jawed at her mother. And for a moment Ida managed a straight face. Then the two women burst into laughter.

"Did I ever thank you for providing a terrific home for us?"

Ida nodded. "Every time you brought me a piece of art to hang on the refrigerator. Every time that den was filled with all your friends."

"Thanks, Mom."

Ida reached for her magazine, idly opened it to a middle page. "You want to talk about the other issue you've been avoiding?"

Kara didn't feign ignorance, but she didn't directly answer the question. "Howard proposed the other day."

Ida's eyebrows rose. "And you told him what?"

"I didn't tell him anything," she said. "He took it back before I had a chance to."

"I suppose he knew you weren't in love with him."

"But then, how can I be in love with Marcus? He's everything I don't want."

"How do you know what you want? You've never let yourself give him much of a chance."

"What were the two of you whispering about the night of Erica's party?"

"The two of who?"

"You and Marcus got awfully quiet when I walked into the kitchen."

Ida shrugged, but didn't meet Kara's eyes. "We've talked about a lot of things. And your father has some more questions about what he has in store for Patrice. She might be twenty-four, but we're still the parents."

"He's going to make her a star," Kara said.

"And that upsets you." It came as a comment, not a question.

Kara chewed on it for a while. "There was a time when I would have said yes."

"And what about now?"

"Patrice has to meet her own destiny. I'm a grant writer who practices psychology on the side," Kara said with a smile. "I like my life."

Ida said not a word.

"I do," Kara said. "Really."

Ida raised a brow.

"And Marcus makes me happy," Kara finally added. "When he's not making me crazy."

"That's what men do. Your father made me crazy. Twice I turned him down when he asked me to marry him. But look at us. It's been thirty-three years and I love him more than ever."

Kara twisted one of her curls. "So you're saying I should what?"

Chuckling, Ida closed the magazine and got up. She kissed Kara on the top of the head. "You're a big girl now, baby. I think you'll figure it out."

* * *

The moving trucks were the next sign that not only had Marcus left Mrs. Abersoll's house, but he wouldn't be returning. From her sunroom window, where she ostensibly sat reading her Sunday-school lesson, Kara watched the moving men load beds, tables and office equipment. The beeping of a large white panel truck made her get up. Backing into the driveway, the truck threatened her flower beds. By the time she got outside and within hollering distance, the driver had corrected the angle of the Portland Piano and Music Company truck.

The toot of a car horn got Kara's attention. She waved at Amber, then joined her.

"What's going on?"

"Our star is moving on," Amber said. "Someone from his office called and said they wouldn't be needing the rest of the meals they'd preordered." Amber grinned. "I get to keep the money, though. I just came by to pick up some cookware and trays I left."

Kara followed Amber into the house, where movers, office supply staff and the piano company people efficiently worked.

"Soon it'll be like no one was ever here," Amber observed as the living room was stripped of its furniture, art and plants.

Had he really left without saying goodbye?

That would have been at least neighborly courtesy. Kara conceded to herself that he didn't owe her any small-town courtesies, neighborly or otherwise. In Los Angeles, as in a lot of large American cities, people didn't know who lived next door or across the street, let alone feel obligated to say goodbye when they left.

And therein lay the problem with loving a man like Marcus Ambrose.

She'd been nothing except a source of entertaining amusement for him during his sojourn in Wayside, much as a cat toys with a trapped bird. And Kara had debuted as the bird.

"Would you like to come over for a cup of coffee?"

Amber shook her head. "Can't today. I'm catering the Wayside Revelers' bingo night. You know how they are about their food. They want a lot of it and on time."

Balancing her load, Amber made it back to her minivan. She tucked the pans into the back and then with Kara watched the piano company people load the heavily padded instrument into the truck.

Amber walked around to the passenger side of her van, reached in the open window and pulled out a white box tied with ribbon.

"Honey pecan rolls?" Kara said, her mouth already watering.

"Not this time. I'm trying out a new recipe for lemon meringue tarts. Tell me what you think."

Slipping the ribbon off, Kara peeked inside, then groaned. "I think I'm going to put in an extra twenty minutes on the treadmill."

"See you later. Oh, did I tell you what else that woman from Marcus's office said?"

"Nadira?" Surely she wasn't back at work the day after her father had died.

Amber shook her head. "No. Not her. Somebody else. She said Marcus just raved about the woman he met here." Amber winked at her. "He called her smart, sassy and beautiful."

Kara's heart did a little flip. He thought she was beautiful.

Joy flooded her spirit. Maybe she hadn't messed things up after all.

Amber got into her van, started the engine and leaned outside the window. "Patrice must have really made an impression on him."

With a wave Amber pulled away.

Kara's elation withered like a rose too long cut from its vine. She blinked back the sudden tears at her eyes and turned to trudge back to her house.

"Excuse me, miss?"

Kara looked at the moving-truck guy, though not really seeing him. Her breaking heart clouded not only her vision but her entire being.

"Can you sign this?"

Kara shook her head. "I'm not connected to that house. I live over here."

She looked at the pathway that connected the two homes. Unnoticed, a gangly weed had sprouted between the stones. Kara bent and yanked it up. Because she didn't get the entire thing, part of the weed remained. She stared at it for a long time, then opened her hand, dropping the stem to the ground.

# *Chapter Fourteen*

The next couple of weeks felt like years. Kara threw herself into her work, but found no satisfaction there. She got confirmation that her application for the JUMP grant had been received and would be processed.

A thank-you note arrived from Nadira, but no mention was made of Marcus. She watched him on the news at the closing gala for the film and music festival and saw Patrice right up front near him.

The rift between the sisters continued despite Kara's efforts at reconciliation. She bought a gift card from Patrice's favorite store, enclosed it with a pretty journal and a note of apology. Kara got silence in return. Patrice didn't even acknowledge the gift. Ida chalked it up to last-minute preparations for the concert and a whirl of activity with Marcus's studio in Los Angeles. Twice now Patrice had been to L.A. But Kara heard the details secondhand, via her mother or her siblings.

The entire town seemed plastered with posters and

hype about the benefit concert sponsored by Community Christian Church. Reverend Baines had taken so many inquiries that they were thinking about adding a second show or possibly moving the performance from the high school auditorium, which held about three hundred, to the football field at the school.

Kara tried to ignore all the hype—it only served to remind her of Marcus. She'd stopped wondering how she'd managed to fall in love with him and focused instead on trying to quick-heal her broken heart.

At the moment she stood in line at the grocery store. Just two of the six checkouts were open, and she found herself in the shorter but slower-moving line behind a woman who had enough milk, diapers and paper towels to open a day-care center.

She reached for a candy bar, then put it back. The multicolored chocolate wrappers beckoned, but she shut out their whispering. In the past few weeks she'd mainlined honey pecan rolls and scarfed down enough junk and comfort food to pack on a couple of extra pounds. Today, however, she'd vowed to get back on the straight and narrow and had put in thirty minutes on the elliptical machine at the fitness center downtown in a good-faith first start.

Without the chocolate fix, she let her gaze roam the other items designed to snare the impulse buyer. Usually she ignored the tabloids in the racks, but one headline caught her eye: Marcus Ambrose Scores A New Beauty.

Praying that no one saw her, Kara glanced around, then plucked the paper from the shelf and flipped through looking for the article. There, on page twenty-seven, next to a feature about liposuction for zoo animals, was Marcus Ambrose mugging for the camera with a sexy, sassy woman clutched to him.

None other than Patrice.

Hands trembling, Kara didn't even bother reading the story. In this case, a picture said it all. Patrice clearly adored the man she snuggled next to. Wearing a red-and-white outfit Kara had never seen, she looked like innocence and sin rolled together in a tempting package that no man would be able to resist, particularly Marcus Ambrose.

"Ma'am, could you put your items on the conveyer belt?"

Kara looked up. Her turn had come. But she no longer wanted any of the items in her basket. All she wanted to do was curl up and cry.

"I've changed my mind," she said. "I'm sorry."

The clerk shrugged, came around and pulled her cart out of the way, motioned for the person behind Kara to move up and snatched up a phone at his register. "Reshelve on aisle three."

Kara pulled a five-dollar bill from her wallet and dropped it on the conveyor belt. In a daze, she walked away.

"Your change, ma'am. You forgot your change."

Kara never heard him.


"Look at it this way," Haley said. "At least you had a couple of fun dates with him. And there's always Howard."

Kara fingered the computer-chip earrings. She'd taken to wearing them as a reminder that *somebody* out there liked her.

"And what about that Ian fellow, the soccer player?"

"He's still laid up with a broken leg and will be for weeks." She shook her head. "I wasn't really interested in dating him. He was just a nice guy. We had things in common."

"So do you and Marcus."

Kara waved the tabloid in front of Haley. "That's my sister's boyfriend."

Scrunching her face up, Haley disagreed. "Something about that just doesn't feel right, Kara. I've listened to everything you've said, but I just can't see Patrice in the role of man-stealing heroine."

"She's not," Kara agreed, leaning back in her chair. "I'm way over that."

"Then what's the problem?"

"I miss my sister," she said miserably. "This is a special time for her and I can't share in her happiness." She didn't need to add that she'd yet to get over Marcus. It wasn't for lack of trying.

"If she won't come to you, go to her."

"I can't just show up in L.A. at his studio demanding to see my sister."

Haley reached into the pocket of her button-down shirt. "You don't have to," she said, handing Kara a ticket.

"What's this?"

"The hottest ticket in town. To the benefit concert. I knew you'd given yours away. This may be your best chance to see Patrice. Matt says she sounds terrific with the choir."

Accepting the ticket, Kara thought about it. Knowing she wouldn't be able to stand seeing Marcus, even though she'd miss her sister's big debut, Kara had given her own front-row tickets to one of the women at the shelter.

Now, though, she'd go to the sold-out show. She'd try to ignore Marcus and find a way to patch things up with Patrice.

The next evening Kara arrived just as the house lights dimmed. She slipped into her seat in the second row.

Someone squeezed her shoulders.

Kara turned around.

"Hey, baby. We're glad you came," Ida said. The entire Spencer clan occupied most of the row behind her. She waved at the twins, who wiggled in their seats, then turned her attention to Cliff, who stood on stage with the mayor.

"We'd like to welcome you to the culmination of sorts of our music and film festival," the mayor said. "We've had a wonderful month of movies, workshops and concerts."

After thanking all of the assorted committee members, the mayor passed the cordless microphone to Cliff, who also thanked people, including the college for opening up its convocation center for the event.

Kara looked stage left toward the curtains where choir members waited to come out. She wondered what might be going through Marcus's mind at the moment.

"I'd like to introduce our guest of honor," Cliff said. "Mr. Marcus Ambrose!"

The crowd came to its feet, cheering, stomping and applauding. Kara rose, too, but so she could see.

After what seemed like a long time, the audience quieted down and settled back into their seats.

"Thank you for that," Marcus said.

Kara realized how much she'd missed hearing his melodic voice, rich and deep.

"You all were great to me during the music and film festival and I'm glad I got the opportunity to come back for this benefit concert. Tonight it's not about me," he said. "This is about giving praises to the One who makes it all possible." He pointed in the air and several people applauded.

"I've had the opportunity to work with some terrific musicians in my day, but let me tell you something, Wayside. You have a treasure right here. Matt, come on out here."

Matt Brandon-Dumaine walked out onto the stage to loud applause led by the Community Christian Church membership.

"I'm a pretty good piano player," Marcus said. "But you ain't heard nothing till you hear this man." The two men clasped in a hug, then began an a cappella praise song.

As they crescendoed, the curtains opened to reveal a grand piano, drums, a reed and horn section and violinists. The choir, all dressed in jeans, white sneakers and matching T-shirts with the Community Christian logo emblazoned on the front, entered from both sides of the stage singing the chorus as they filled the risers.

Matt and Marcus segued into another song, this time with music, and brought the crowd to its feet.

The concert went on for forty minutes with a combination of praise and worship tunes and original ones. They sang some of Matt's hits from his days as a gospel recording artist. And Kara recognized some of the music from the tape Marcus had let her listen to.

"Show some love to the Community Christian Church Mass Choir," Marcus said at a standing mike. He talked while the choir exited the stage.

"I've been singing for a long time now," he said. "And you always meet people who want to be singers, people who are willing to do anything—" He nodded his head and quirked his mouth. "And I mean *anything*," he added, to the snickers of some in the audience, "to get a recording contract. But every now and then you meet someone truly remarkable. Someone with extraordinary talent."

"Ooh, this is Patrice," Ida whispered loudly.

Marcus laughed. "Yes, Mrs. Spencer. This is your daughter. Ladies and gentlemen, I'd like to introduce to you Miss Patrice Spencer."

All the Spencers jumped up, including Kara, applauding wildly. Patrice waved to them and blew a kiss as she joined Marcus. He took her hand in his, and spoke directly to the audience.

"This young woman's voice blew me away the first time I heard it. I was so impressed, I signed her up to sing on my next CD. It'll be released in about six months, but I'm not gonna wait that long to share her with you. If you've never had the opportunity to hear her sing, you're in for a treat."

He kissed her on the cheek and walked to the piano. Patrice positioned herself nearby and stood at the standing microphone.

"Thank you all for coming tonight," she said. "The song I'm going to sing was written by a very talented songwriter who hasn't been given the recognition she deserves."

Marcus began the piano intro.

Goose bumps jumped out all along Kara's skin.

She recognized the music. Recognized it because she'd written it. Her gaze flew to Patrice.

"Some of you already know my sister Kara. She's a psychologist and volunteers everywhere in town. But mostly she's the best big sister a girl could ask for. I count it a blessing to be able to sing her music for you tonight."

Patrice opened up and sang the house down. By the time she finished singing and Marcus finished playing, there wasn't a dry eye in the building.

Patrice took her bows, then ran down the stage steps and embraced Kara, the spotlights shining on them.

Ida joined her daughters and someone passed up tissues to the three women.

On stage, Marcus still sat at the piano. "When I came to Wayside, one of the first people I met was Dr. Kara Spencer. She pushed me, defied me and challenged me."

Kara wiped her eyes and stood with her arms around her sister and mother, staring at Marcus.

"What she doesn't know is that she also captured my heart."

Kara's eyes widened. The audience oohed. Ida squeezed her waist.

"For somebody who has made a living singing love songs, you'd think I'd know how to tell the woman I love how much she means to me."

If Ida and Patrice hadn't been holding on to her, Kara's knees would have buckled beneath her.

"But I'm not very good at one-to-one conversations. I know how to express myself in words that are in song. So, Kara, this is for you."

Kara knew her legs were carrying her toward him,

but she couldn't feel a thing. She came to a halt at the edge of the stage. Not a sound could be heard in the convocation center.

Marcus then poured out his heart to Kara in a love song written just for her. He lifted the microphone from the stand and picked up a single long-stemmed rose from the piano. By the time he finished the song he stood in front of Kara and offered her the rose. The crowd went wild.

Kara was crying all over again.

Spotlights shone on both of them. In front of a packed auditorium Marcus got down on one knee. "Kara, you're the reason I sing. I love you more than I thought it possible to love another person. Will you give me another chance? Will you marry me?"

She nodded.

"What'd she say?" someone from way in the back hollered out.

He chuckled. "I don't think all these witnesses heard that."

"Yes!" Kara said. And then she was in his arms, right where she wanted to be all the time.

# *Epilogue*

"I have a confession to make," Marcus said.

"What's that?"

It was the second Sunday, and Kara and Marcus were headed to dinner at Ida and Gordon's. His work schedule kept him pretty tied up, so his trips to Wayside to visit Kara had been few and far between in the past six weeks. But Kara had traveled to L.A., where she saw Patrice record the songs for Marcus's gospel CD in his studio.

He pulled up behind Faye and Wade's minivan and cut the engine.

"You know that grant you applied for? The JUMP grant."

Kara glanced over at him. "Umm-hmm. What about it?"

He took a deep breath. "Well, I didn't tell you, but I'm the JUMP Foundation."

"I know," Kara said as she unbuckled her seat belt.

Marcus frowned. "What do you mean, you know? It's supposed to be a secret. Nobody knows."

Kara grinned at him. If there'd ever really been a challenge between them, Marcus had won it hands down. The private Marcus shielded from public view all the work he did behind the scenes, charitable and philanthropic work that benefited mostly young people—those at risk just as he'd once been.

"Nadira may be your assistant," Kara said, "but she's also counted among *my* friends these days."

"You've suborned my staff."

She laughed at his wounded expression. "Not at all. We've just developed friendships. Besides," Kara said, "I needed to know what it meant to be a part of your world."

"So she told you all of my secrets?"

Kara grinned. "Yep."

Marcus's answering smile warmed her. "And have I told you how much I love you?"

Kara glanced at her watch. "Not in the last thirty minutes."

"I love you, Dr. Kara."

"I love you, too, Marcus Ambrose."

They shared a kiss, a slow and thoughtful embrace that quickly blossomed into something stronger. Marcus opened his door. "I think we need to go inside."

"Th-that sounds like a good idea."

Hand in hand they headed up the walkway to the front door and the frenzy of a second-Sunday dinner.

"You know what else?" Marcus told her.

"What?" Kara said, a smile at her mouth.

"I haven't had a headache since the day you agreed to marry me. But can we maybe move the wedding date up a few months? I'd like to get to the honeymoon part.''

Kara's laughter rang out, the sound a harmonious melody in the cool afternoon. ''You'll just have to wait, Mr. Ambrose. You'll just have to wait.''

\* \* \* \* \*

Dear Reader,

Greetings to you. Thank you for reading
*Sweet Harmony,* my second Love Inspired novel.
I truly appreciated all of the wonderful letters you
sent following the release of Haley and Matt's story
in *Sweet Accord.*

The fictional town of Wayside, Oregon, is, as you
may have guessed, a very special place. I hope you've
also enjoyed my forays into this slice of small-town
Americana. I've traveled to the Portland, Oregon, area
many times and fell in love with the green spaces, the
clean air and the history of the state.

Amber Montgomery's story is next in *Sweet Devotion,*
which will be published in Steeple Hill's new trade
paperback program next month (February 2004).
Amber has had a difficult life, and her faith journey is
one of trials and ultimate triumph. Please join me in
celebrating her path to freedom in my first Steeple Hill
single title. An excerpt is included here to whet your
appetite.

And in case you're wondering, yes, that flirtatious
songbird Patrice Spencer, Kara's younger sister, has
her own story in the works. More details to come
on that one.

In the meantime, I can be reached at P.O. Box 1438,
Dept. SH, Yorktown, VA 23692.

May God's richest blessings continue to be yours,

Felicia Mason

Yorktown, Virginia

*Coming Next Month*

*SWEET DEVOTION*

*Things start off on the wrong foot and go downhill when gourmet chef Amber Montgomery encounters Wayside's new police chief, a single dad with marriage on his mind and order to restore to an out-of-control church camp. It'll take more than arts and crafts in the afternoon and songs around a bonfire to renew Amber's spirit...or to make her realize that love heals the wounds of the past.*

*Here's a sneak peek at Felicia Mason's next Steeple Hill novel featuring Wayside, Oregon, and Community Christian Church. Look for Amber and Paul's inspiring love story in February, 2004.*

Armed with a carving knife, Amber Montgomery took cover as a metal folding chair hurtled her way. The chair crashed against the edge of a white-draped carving table, taking out the end of the serving station where she'd been carving beef at the Wayside Revelers' annual dinner dance.

She watched in horror as eight pounds of beets splattered to the floor, sending deep red beet juice splashing up and out like a demented geyser.

She'd known, of course, that taking this catering job carried a certain amount of risk. The Wayside Revelers tended to revel a bit too much at their functions. But after their last fiasco at the VFW hall, Amber thought they'd mellowed and would be on their best behavior tonight.

That, obviously, wasn't the case.

She didn't know how this melee had started, but she needed to—

"Watch out!" someone yelled.

Amber ducked a moment before another chair came within inches of taking *her* out.

This was getting personal!

She jumped up. "Hey, I'm the caterer. Why are you attacking me?"

But no one heard her or paid any attention. They were too busy destroying the hall and themselves—and having a great time doing so. The scene in front of her looked like a barroom brawl in the wild, wild West. Except this wasn't the 1800s frontier. It was peaceful little Wayside, Oregon, population 17,800.

Over the melee, Amber heard what sounded like police sirens. Help was on the way!

Maybe she could salvage the trays of lemon meringue tarts—six hours of work. Amber inched toward the desserts, but someone spied them at the same time. The elderly man grabbed one in each hand and smiled.

"Don't you have any respect for food?"

Unmindful of the havoc playing out behind him, the man shook his head, grinned a toothless smile and aimed.

"Don't you dare!" Amber said, holding her hands up in front of her face.

"Lighten up, honey," he said. "It's just a pastry."

The words registered a moment before her own lemon meringue hit her in the face.

Amber shrieked and whirled around.

"Hold it right there."

With one hand Amber wiped pie from her face, while the other dropped the carving knife she'd been clutching.

She cleared her vision enough to spot the pie thrower scuttling off to the side and disappearing into the crowd. She wiped away more meringue, and the shadow in front of her came into focus, the details registering.

Tall with broad shoulders, a slim waist and feet planted apart, he scowled at her and eyed the knife she'd dropped. A very big, very angry cop stood not three feet in front of her.

''You're under arrest, lady.''

# A brand-new lyrical novel
# from award-winning author

# FELICIA
# MASON

"Mason is a
superb storyteller...
She creates magic."
—*Publishers Weekly*

*Available February 2004,
wherever books are sold.*

---

Visit us at www.steeplehill.com

SSD511US-MM